She knew the truth too late.

Carson and his children would be too easy to love. She had to get away.

"I'm going to town. There's the…" *Think, think.* "Stuff. At the…feed store."

Carson quirked a brow. "Maybe I'll go with you. The kids and I need some…stuff, too."

She wanted to protest. But the challenge in his eyes wouldn't let her.

"I'll go get ready."

She turned to leave, but he reached out for her. "Kylie, we really don't need anything in town."

She knew that. He'd been teasing, trying to get the best of her. And just for a brief moment she'd hoped he wanted to spend time with her.

She might have been the first girl he kissed, the girl he promised to always love, but, she reminded herself, she wasn't the woman he married.

She realized her mistake. She'd been thinking of him as that boy she'd loved. He wasn't. Not anymore.

She had fallen for a memory.

And the memory had turned to hope.

Brenda Minton lives in the Ozarks with her husband, children, cats, dogs and strays. She is a pastor's wife, Sunday-school teacher, coffee addict and sleep deprived. Not in that order. Her dream to be an author for Harlequin started somewhere in the pages of a romance novel about a young American woman stranded in a Spanish castle. Her dreams came true, and twenty-plus books later, she is an author hoping to inspire young girls to dream.

Books by Brenda Minton

Love Inspired

Mercy Ranch

Reunited with the Rancher

Bluebonnet Springs

Second Chance Rancher
The Rancher's Christmas Bride
The Rancher's Secret Child

Martin's Crossing

A Rancher for Christmas
The Rancher Takes a Bride
The Rancher's Second Chance
The Rancher's First Love
Her Rancher Bodyguard
Her Guardian Rancher

Visit the Author Profile page at Harlequin.com for more titles.

Reunited with the Rancher

Brenda Minton

Recycling programs for this product may not exist in your area.

ISBN-13: 978-1-335-42830-1

Reunited with the Rancher

This edition published by arrangement with Love Inspired Books.

www.Harlequin.com

Printed in U.S.A.

To appoint unto them that mourn in Zion, to give unto them beauty for ashes, the oil of joy for mourning, the garment of praise for the spirit of heaviness; that they might be called trees of righteousness, the planting of the Lord, that he might be glorified.

—*Isaiah* 61:3

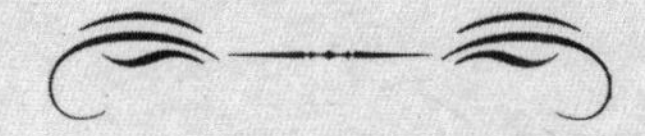

This book is dedicated to the men and women who proudly serve in our armed forces, and to their families. We value your sacrifice and your bravery. May God richly bless you and keep you in all of your endeavors.

Chapter One

Carson West had a plan. He had a plan to walk up to his father, hand him back the letter he'd sent—offering him a job as the physician of a clinic in Hope, Oklahoma—and tell him "Not in this lifetime." No way would he give up the opportunity he'd been offered in Chicago for a job in a town that had seen better days fifty years ago.

No way would he settle in the town his mother had fled twenty years ago. She had taken her three children and nothing else. They hadn't even been allowed to pack a suitcase. They hadn't told friends they were leaving. They'd just gone in the middle of the night, like thieves fleeing the scene of the crime.

It seemed like a lifetime ago, but today he was back and he planned on letting Jack West know how it had felt to lose a father, even one who had randomly yelled, drank until he passed out, or woke them up at night with nightmares no one could sleep through. Because of his two tours in Vietnam, those behaviors hadn't been in Jack's control. But letting his family go without ever trying to contact them? Carson did blame him for that.

As he eased his SUV up the drive of the once rundown farm, he noticed several obvious differences. The white farmhouse with faded paint had been remodeled. The garage appeared to now be apartments. A short distance away stood a log home with stone trim and an attached three-car garage.

He'd been thirteen when they left, and it hadn't been easy leaving this place. His father had been tough, sometimes angry, never predictable, but he'd still been their father. After a while Carson had buried the best of his memories and tried to push this place from his mind.

But after all of these years, had he expected to find it unchanged? Had he expected the old dog Pete to still be sleeping on the front porch? Did he think there would still be the same overgrown lawn, broken-down tractors and aging farm trucks?

Instead of finding the farm he remembered, he saw a place that had become something completely different. Most significantly, there had been a sign at the front of the property welcoming him to Mercy Ranch.

Carson slowed as he drove past the house but kept going, in the direction of the supersized and modern stable that stood where the old barn used to be. He could see people milling about and guessed it would be the best place to find Jack.

He parked, ignoring the curious glances of the men who were pulling sacks of grain from the back of a truck and carrying them inside. He got out and opened the passenger door of the Escalade. His daughter, Maggie, grinned up at him, her blond ringlets sticking to her face where she'd gotten sticky with juice. Almost three years old, she giggled often and jabbered nonstop. Her brown eyes were warm and her nose pert. She looked just like Anna, and each time he realized that, it hurt. Not as much as it had at first, but the pain was definitely still there.

He unbuckled her from the car seat and she held out her arms to him. As he settled her on his left side, she patted his arm and reminded him to get her brother, Andy.

His son Andy would be five in six months and he was Maggie's complete opposite. With Carson's dark hair and gray eyes, he was the serious one, quiet, always watching, always thinking.

Even now his gaze focused on the window, his eyes narrowing as he surveyed this new place.

Carson pocketed the letter from his father and helped his son out of the SUV. In the arena a couple of horses and riders worked cattle with the late afternoon sun beating down on them. He could hear calves calling for their mamas and a horse whinnying somewhere in the distance. It was the sounds of Carson's youth, and yet nothing appeared to be the same since when his mom had taken them away.

Carson beat back his anger. He guessed that sentiment had been on low heat since he'd left Dallas that morning, heading north to Hope. What a ridiculous name for a washed-out resort town with tumbledown buildings, no stoplights and bad memories. Hope. There was no hope here.

The only thing here was the past. And he'd come home to confront it, to confront his father.

Carson, his brother Colt and little sister Daisy were all jacked up because of this place, the man who lived here and the past.

"Hello?" He heard a soft voice from behind him.

"Hi," Maggie said as she peeked over his shoulder. She patted his arm to get his attention. "Daddy. Look."

Andy, ever unsure of strangers, had climbed

out of the SUV and was holding tight to his leg. Carson did an awkward turn, holding one child in his arms while the other clung to his jeans like they were a lifeline. His gaze dropped to the woman who barely reached his shoulder. Light brown hair lifted in the breeze and drifted across her face.

A Labrador puppy tumbled around her feet, nipping her ankles and pulling at the laces on her shoes.

She was country pretty, with freckles sprinkled across her nose, no makeup, wide hazel eyes and a heart-deep smile.

"Can I help you?" she said in a way that made him want to tell her everything. His secrets. Fears. Dreams. It unsettled him and made him a little angry. With her. That wasn't logical and he liked logic.

Besides, she belonged here. That automatically put her on the wrong side.

"I'm here to see Jack."

"He's in the barn. I can take you." She started to turn away from him.

"I think I can find him on my own."

"Of course you can." She bit down on her lip as she studied him, then turned her attention to his children. A smile tugged the corners of her mouth. "Perhaps I should take them inside while you go find him."

He looked from the woman to his children. She was a stranger to them. It didn't matter that she had sun-kissed highlights in her brown hair, and golden hazel eyes that danced with laughter. It didn't matter that her expression changed as she studied Andy, who was now staring off at the horizon, tapping his fingers against his leg in time to music that couldn't be heard.

"Thank you for the offer but we're only here for a few minutes. Long enough to talk to my… to Jack." As he said it, he caught Andy's expression as he focused on the puppy.

It had been a long day, and the last few weeks had been difficult with the house selling so quickly and then packing all of their belongings. No, not everything. Packing had been a time of letting go. It hadn't been easy to give Anna's stuff to her sisters, to watch as they went through things, smiling and sharing memories. Thirty-two months had passed since her death. It had been time to let go. More than time.

"I'll walk with you," the woman at his side said with a slight lift of her chin. "In case you change your mind."

Change his mind about what? Her help? Or talking to Jack?

He took off his sunglasses and looked at her, trying to decide if he should know her. As they stood there, squared off and unmoving, Andy dropped to his knees and began to pet the puppy. Maggie squirmed to be free. They'd been in the car for hours. A twinge of guilt forced him to take a deep breath. He lowered Maggie to the ground and she giggled as the puppy immediately began to lick her face.

"No, don't." He tried to stop the puppy and the little girl. Both ignored him.

"They're having fun. Maybe give them—and yourself—a minute. I'm sure you're all about whatever it is you have to say to Jack, but it won't hurt to count to ten."

"I've been counting to ten for a long time."

"Carson, I know this is what you think needs to be done. I really do understand." She said it with compassion and a knowing sadness in her eyes.

And then he realized she had called him by name, acting as if she knew something about his life. "Do we know one another?"

She dimpled at the question. "Well, don't I feel special? And here I believed it when you told me you would always love me."

He studied her, trying to picture a younger version of her. He had pushed memories of this town and this ranch to the back of his mind for so many years. He'd blocked bad memories and refused to think of the good ones. And now it seemed there was a memory he should have held on to.

A sharp *woof* sent Andy scampering back with a startled cry. He grabbed Carson's legs and held tight as Maggie giggled at the puppy who crouched, his tail wagging. Ever cautious, Andy reached his fingers toward the animal.

"Don't worry. Skip is a good puppy. He likes to play chase." The still-nameless woman shifted her attention from him and knelt in front of Andy, grimacing as she did.

Carson glanced from his children to the stable a short distance away. Over the years he'd learned patience. Patience had made him a top surgeon. Patience, and noticing things, noticing people. It was often more about what they didn't say than what they did.

Today he felt as if his patience might be in short supply.

Next to him the woman struggled to rise to her feet. Without thinking, Carson held out a hand to help her. She hesitated, and he saw the spark of something in her gaze. Not distrust. Pride. He recognized it because he'd been there. For nearly three years he'd been giving that same look to anyone who offered him help. Her hand grasped his and he pulled her to her feet.

He held on to her hand and she looked up. As

he held it, his memories took him down back roads to quiet summer days when he was thirteen.

"I want to see Jack and then I'm leaving. I'm not here for a family reunion."

She wiggled her hand free. "I understand. I just wanted to give your little boy a moment to catch his breath. I'm sure he's had a long and overwhelming day."

"He has." Carson left out the part about his son having a long and overwhelming three years. No, not quite three years. Thirty-two months. It had been thirty-two months since Anna said she had to run to the store. Thirty-two months since he'd been sitting at the kitchen table, waiting for her to come home as sirens sounded in the distance.

Thirty-two months since the knock at the door telling him his pregnant wife had been taken to the hospital after a hit-and-run accident.

He lifted Maggie and she hooked her arms around his neck. Andy remained close to his side, but sneaked an occasional look at the puppy that had plopped to his belly, his chin resting on Andy's shoes.

The woman standing too close for comfort laughed a little as Andy wiggled his foot and the puppy immediately returned to play mode.

Her laughter dragged him down another path. Memories crashed into the present as the breeze kicked up, bringing with it the scent of September rain and a hint of coconut shampoo. Like it or not, today had become a day of reunions.

He remembered. This woman had once been the girl who'd lived just down the road and they'd ridden bikes together. They'd gone swimming in the creek. They'd shared secrets neither had felt comfortable telling anyone else. She'd been Kylie Adams back then. And her hair had been more blond than brown.

She'd become one of the many memories he'd pushed deep down, because forgetting was easier than remembering. Until today. Today he remembered her. He remembered that summer when two kids had discovered something sweet. He'd kissed her. A sweet but clumsy first kiss. And he'd told her someday he'd marry her.

He met her gaze and he saw the twinkle of amusement, because she knew he'd finally remembered. Now he had a second reason for regretting the decision to return to Hope. The last thing he wanted, or needed, were more memories.

"Kylie. It's been a long time."

Kylie had recognized the second Carson remembered her. She'd been waiting for it since the moment he'd taken off his sunglasses and looked at her, unsure, measured, trying to get his bearings.

Twenty years had slipped away as he'd given her that look, confident and unsure all mixed together. She'd had to remind herself he was no longer the boy who'd promised to rescue her. She was no longer the girl from the trailer park who needed rescuing. She had rescued herself and built a new life here, in Oklahoma. In Hope.

He had lost his wife. She had lost her husband. They had that in common. They'd both been widowed too young and too soon.

"I guess it would be pointless to say I didn't expect to see you here." He surveyed the homes, the stable, the white vinyl rail fences. "I guess I didn't expect any of this."

"I'm sure you didn't. Things are seldom what we think."

He sighed, and she felt for him. She knew that he had been blindsided by all of this.

He scrubbed a hand through short, dark hair and glanced toward the pasture, a man trying to get his bearings. He obviously didn't know that his father had reinvented the ranch. It was a place of new beginnings. A place of mercy.

"Why are you here?" he asked, his tone cool.

"You'll have to ask your dad. He's in his office." She reached but her hand dropped short of touching his arm that held Maggie. "I'm sure this is the last place you want to be. But if you'll talk to him…"

"I think this was a mistake. I should have kept on driving."

Carson West rocked that firm foundation just a little.

"Don't go," she encouraged, even though she knew it would be better for her if he left. She knew Jack needed this. And Carson did, too, even if he didn't believe it. "Friend to friend, stay and talk to him."

He pulled his sunglasses from his pocket and pushed them on. She was struck again by his masculine beauty. She remembered the same reaction from years ago. He'd been thirteen and beautiful with his suntanned skin, smoky gray eyes and slightly longer dark hair. Twenty years later his beauty was more masculine with a strong jawline, cheekbones that were defined and eyes that were more serious than laughing.

She held a hand out to Andy and the little boy took it, unsure, a little lost. They started forward, and she left it for Carson to follow or not.

"What are you doing?" Carson called out as she put distance between them.

She wished she had an answer to that question. It felt like stepping into quicksand. But for this moment, she could put aside the instinct to fight or flee and she could help Jack make peace with at least one of his children.

She glanced back at Carson. He hadn't moved. He was still standing there with his daughter in his arms looking unsure. She thought it was not a familiar emotion for him. Uncertainty.

"I'm taking you to the stable to see your father. I might as well go along. Someone has to be there to referee."

He laughed a little but didn't deny it. And then he moved forward, catching up with them.

As they approached the barn, Jack West emerged from the door. He was as tall as Carson, a little broader through the shoulders, but his strength seemed to diminish a little more each day. He pulled off his cowboy hat and put a trembling hand through shaggy gray hair as he watched the four of them walking toward him.

"Carson?" His voice shook a bit. From emotion or Parkinson's, Kylie couldn't tell.

"In the flesh." Carson stopped a good ten feet from his father.

"I guess this isn't a social call?" Jack grinned as he said it, though sadness lingered in his eyes, as well. "You're not here to accept my offer?"

"It isn't a social call, Jack, and I'm definitely not here to accept your offer. I came to tell you that we did just fine without you. I graduated from medical school and I'm a trauma surgeon.

I have two children. And in case you've wondered, Daisy and Colt survived, too."

"I know they have." Jack pointed to his office. "Let's step in here and talk. We don't need for everyone to be in our business."

"We can say what has to be said right here, and then I'm leaving."

"Don't be so stubborn," Jack shot back.

"I'm not stubborn. What I have to say won't take two minutes. I'm not going to discuss this job you're offering or any excuses you might have."

"I don't have excuses, I only have the truth."

Kylie shook her head at Jack, trying to at least get him to back down. She could feel the trembling that was radiating from Andy's thin little frame, his hand quivering while it was snug in hers. Jack sighed and nodded, his gaze settling on his grandson.

The little boy didn't want to be involved in this argument any more than Kylie did. She wanted to walk away from Jack, Carson and the two children, because if she walked away she wouldn't have to get involved. If she walked away she wouldn't have to look at Carson's children and have her heart ask the question *what if*?

There were no what-ifs in her life anymore; there was only cold, harsh reality.

"We have to talk," Jack agreed. "But not right now. Not like this. Not standing here in a dusty barnyard. Not with your children watching."

"You're right." Carson took a step back from his father and slowly looked from his daughter clinging to his neck to the little boy standing next to Kylie. His expression softened. "We'll just say our goodbyes and if I'm ever in the area again, I'll look you up."

"You've already had a long day," Jack said. "Might as well stay for supper. Give Maggie and Andy a chance to rest."

Carson reached for his son's hand. Kylie wondered if he noticed that his dad used his children's names. If only Jack would tell him the truth. About everything. But that would mean opening himself up. Men were so stubborn.

She knew firsthand how stubborn a man could be. They didn't open up. They didn't ask for help. They kept everything inside until... She blinked back tears, unwilling to go down the path to her own painful past.

"I'm on a tight schedule. I have a job interview in Chicago in three days. We have a hotel reservation in Missouri for tonight."

"Mercy Ranch is almost a hotel," Jack said with humor.

"I'm not staying a single night on this ranch."

Carson said the words sharply, and the little girl in his arms leaned back, her eyes widening.

Carson closed his eyes and drew in a breath. He leaned in to his daughter and whispered that he was sorry. Andy and Maggie needed to be rescued from this situation, just until the men talked and worked out their differences. Not that she expected them to be able to do that in a five-minute conversation.

"I'm taking your children to the house."

Carson looked shocked at her announcement. She was just as shocked. Getting involved in this was the last thing she wanted to do. What she wanted was to keep her world nice and safe without having it stirred up. She loved her life on this ranch. She had dealt with her past, both distant and recent. She'd come to terms with the things she couldn't change. For the first time in her life she was truly happy.

And now Carson West was here shaking things up and threatening that happiness. But his children were innocent, and she couldn't let them stay and witness their father and grandfather working out their differences.

She reached for Maggie and the little girl willingly shifted herself to Kylie's arms. Carson held on for a moment, but then released his daughter. With Maggie situated on one hip, she held out her free hand to Andy. He took it, though he looked unsure.

She didn't blame him. She was a little bit unsure herself. Actually, she wasn't unsure at all. Carson back in Hope, back in her life, wasn't what she'd expected or wanted. She'd known Jack's plans for the new medical clinic in Hope. The doctor originally hired had worked for only a month, then decided he wanted something different.

For some reason she hadn't thought about Carson for the job. She'd thought it would be another nice, safe stranger. Someone she didn't remember for the sweetest first kiss, or promises he'd made to a girl who would have given anything to escape her life.

It could have been anyone other than Carson West.

Not the one man who could undo everything she'd built.

Chapter Two

Carson watched as Kylie walked away with his children. When he turned around, Jack had walked off. His hand trembled as he reached for a lead rope and unlatched a stall. Carson stepped aside as his father led a horse to the center aisle. The gelding sidestepped a bit and tried to pull back on the lead rope. Jack held him tight and crosstied him.

"What are you doing?" Carson asked.

"What I had planned on doing before you came stomping in here bent on retribution. I have a buyer coming to look at this gelding and I plan on having him ready to be looked at."

"That horse is mean." Carson eyed the animal as he stomped, trying to be free of the lines that held him steady while Jack brushed him out.

"Yeah, he is. But the fella buying him doesn't

care. He works cattle and he says he'll ride it out of him."

"I didn't come here to talk about horses," Carson reminded his father. "I came to tell you I'm not interested in your clinic. I'm not interested in whatever other way you want to make amends for what you did to me. To us. You had no interest in us for twenty years. Don't start now."

"I'm not starting now," Jack said as he brushed the sleek red neck of the horse. "I thought you might like a change of pace so I sent you the offer. The least you could do is stay here and take a look at the clinic."

Stay and be tied to Jack. The next thought took him by surprise. He couldn't stay here and face Kylie each day either. And he had a feeling if he was on this ranch, she'd be here, too. All hazel eyes and sunshine smiles. He still pictured her as a kid of thirteen, laughing, riding bikes, swimming in the creek. She'd changed. But hadn't they all?

The ranch had changed, too. Not just the obvious: new cabins, new stable, new livestock and fancy fences. The name had changed, too. Mercy Ranch. Mercy. He did wonder about the name change. From the Rocking W to Mercy Ranch.

"Why Mercy Ranch?" he asked.

"Mercy," Jack said as he stroked the back of the horse with a soft-bristled brush. *"Mercy* means to offer forgiveness when it is in one's power to punish."

"I know the definition of the word. Why did you rename your family ranch?"

Jack grinned at him. "Because of *mercy.* I didn't deserve it, but I received it. And now I can pay that forward. All of the men and women you see on this ranch are wounded warriors. Military veterans. It's a place for them to start over. Or a place to settle down. It's about mercy. Even the mercy we show ourselves."

"Kylie?"

"Her story is her business. I can only tell you my story." Jack grimaced and dropped the brush he'd been using on the horse. "Well, this is bad timing."

Carson stepped forward, saw the lines of pain in his father's face and the perspiration beading across his brow. "Jack?"

Jack slid a bottle from his pocket and managed with shaking hands to get the lid off. Carson took the pill bottle from him and shook one into his hand. With a sigh Jack put the pill under his tongue and he didn't object when Carson led him to the office where there were several chairs.

"You need to sit down. We don't want you

standing up as your blood pressure decreases. You'll end up facedown on the floor."

"Kylie will think you knocked me out."

"Yeah, right. I'm prone to violence. I'm calling 911." Carson pulled his phone out.

"You'll do no such thing," Jack growled. "I'm fine. Give me a minute. While we wait, you can finish that horse and put him back in the stall."

Carson reached for Jack's wrist and felt his pulse. Rapid but steady. "How often does this happen?"

"Often enough that I need pills. Go take care of the horse." He took a deep breath. "Please."

"I'll put him in the stall."

"Too citified now to do some chores?" Jack badgered as Carson left the office.

Carson gave the horse a quick brushing. He was untying him when another man came walking down the aisle. He appeared to be in his late twenties. He was tall, walked with an easy gait and when he got closer, Carson saw that he had silver-gray eyes. Those eyes pinned Carson with an angry stare.

Carson focused on the eyes rather than how much the younger man looked like him, looked like his brother Colt. He told himself it was coincidence. Plenty of people had gray eyes. That didn't make them related. Right?

"Where's Jack?" the younger man asked.

Carson led the horse to the stall. "He's in his office."

"Jack?" the other man called out, walking past Carson, shoulder checking him as he went.

"Nice to meet you, too," Carson muttered as he followed him to the office. "He can't walk back to the house. Is there a wheelchair around here? Or we can carry him."

"I can walk," Jack growled. "Isaac can help me."

Isaac, the gray-eyed stranger had a name.

Carson motioned toward the door. "Be my guest. Isaac will pick you up when you fall on your face."

"You wouldn't make a good local doctor. You need a better bedside manner."

Carson tamped down on a smile. "Right. I guess I'm a chip off the old block."

They sat there for a minute staring each other down, then Jack sighed. "Isaac, I'm afraid he's right. These old legs are too shaky for that walk back to the house."

"I'll get a wheelchair." Isaac headed toward the door. "Say one thing to upset him and you'll answer to me."

Carson didn't bother to respond. He waited until the other man—Isaac—was gone before he approached Jack again. "I assume you've been to a specialist?"

"Yeah, I have. It's nothing major."

"I would beg to differ, but what do I know. I'm only a doctor."

"Without a bedside manner." Jack closed his eyes and leaned back in the chair. "For what it's worth, I'm sorry."

"It doesn't matter."

"It does matter," Jack said. "Stay here for a few days. We can talk."

"I don't think so." Now, knowing Jack was sick, Carson didn't have the heart for the confrontation. He'd come here expecting the same ranch, the same Jack West, and nothing was what he'd expected.

He pulled a chair close and a moment later Kylie appeared pushing a wheelchair. Carson looked behind her, then he looked to Isaac, looming just inside the door. "Where are my kids?"

Kylie pushed the chair close. "They're with Eve. Don't worry. She's watching them. I just thought it would be easier to do this if they weren't here. And less traumatic for them."

He didn't leave his children with strangers. For good reason. Kylie must have seen something in his expression, because she sighed.

"Carson, they're safe. I promise."

"Of course they are." He glanced at his watch

and opened the pill bottle again. "Time for a second dose."

"You take a second dose," Jack grumbled, but he took the second pill.

"Well, that's a good sign," Kylie said as she slid an arm behind Jack to help him up out of the chair. "Come on, Oscar."

"I'm not a grouch." Jack managed a half grin as he said it.

"Yes, you are." Kylie smoothed Jack's hair and gave him a thorough looking over. "You sure you're okay?"

"I'm good."

"I'll help him get up." Isaac took over, lifting Jack to his feet and helping him into the wheelchair.

"Getting old stinks," Jack said. His voice was weaker than it had been.

Carson reached for his wrist and felt for a pulse.

"Still have a heart?" Jack asked.

"You're not funny," Kylie whispered, with tears in her eyes.

Carson averted his attention and looked down at Jack. "You do still have a heart. But I think it would be good to get you to the house and get you in bed."

It took ten minutes to get Jack back and settled in his recliner in the living room. He insisted he would be most comfortable in the big leather chair. Kylie brought him water and something for the headache, brought on by the nitroglycerin.

Carson was checking Jack's blood pressure with a monitor Kylie had given him when Isaac appeared with Maggie and Andy. Maggie had her arms around Isaac's neck and she jabbered, telling him a story that he probably couldn't make much sense of. Andy followed, but he was expressionless as he tapped a steady rhythm on his leg, a sure sign he was distressed by the unfamiliar situation and place.

He had to get them somewhere and get them settled. Soon. Andy needed a stable place, his things around him, structure. The only way to provide that was to get where they were going as quickly as possible, and find a home where they could start over.

As he considered his next move, the puppy that had been with Kylie appeared. It immediately went to Andy, and Carson watched as his son dropped to the floor and put his arms around the animal. Andy's features relaxed and he smiled as he pulled the puppy close and buried his face in its yellow fur.

Maggie gave the dog a few pats, then she toddled up to Carson. He lifted her and she leaned in to whisper in his ear, "Potty."

"The bathroom is through the kitchen and next to the utility room," Kylie offered. "I can show you."

"Thank you. We'll take care of that and then we need to get on the road. I want to be in a hotel before bedtime."

"No." Andy spoke quietly, his face pressed against the dog.

"Andy?" Carson reached for his son, but Andy pulled back, shaking his head.

"I don't want to go."

"But we have to." Carson shifted, putting himself clearly in his son's line of vision.

Andy looked up, suddenly focused. He shook his head and pulled the Labrador puppy close. "No. I want to stay."

Carson paused at the unexpected outburst from his son. Because Andy was on the autism spectrum, even though it was mild, he rarely put more than a few words together.

The puppy seemed to be the key.

"I'm sorry, Andy, but we can't stay."

Andy shook his head again. Carson became aware of Kylie moving closer. Briefly her hand touched his arm. He looked up and she smiled, thoroughly undoing something inside him that he'd been holding together for thirty-two long months. Now wasn't the most opportune time for him to remember that he had once loved holding a woman close. A teenager, he reminded himself. They'd been little more than kids when they'd known one another. They'd held hands, made up impossible dreams for the future, and then it had ended.

"Andy could take a walk with Skip before you go," Kylie suggested. "It'll give him a chance to unwind, get some fresh air. It might make it easier for him to get back in the car. I'll take him down to see the new calves while you change Maggie."

Kylie held a hand out to Andy and he watched his son slip his small hand in to hers. He'd just been taken by surprise again.

Kylie led Andy out the back door and down the steps. The little boy seemed to be keeping his focus on Skip, and the more he did, the less he tapped at his leg.

"Do you like to swing?" she asked as they crossed the lawn in the direction of the swing Jack had maintained with fresh ropes and the occasional new board. The swing, always a reminder that a long time ago there had been children on this ranch.

Now there were veterans, both men and women. They worked on the ranch with the cattle, with horses Jack raised, and even with the dogs. They were also learning new skills doing construction projects in town.

Kylie glanced down at the little boy holding her hand. He glanced in the direction of the swing and then his gaze briefly shifted to meet hers. He nodded in answer to her question.

"I think your daddy played on this swing when he was a little boy. Would you like for me to push you on it?"

Again he nodded.

When they got to the swing, she lifted him to the seat and showed him how to hold tightly to the rope. She gave him a push and his hands tightened even more. The next time she pushed a little easier and noticed that he relaxed.

As she pushed the swing she told him about the ranch and about knowing his daddy when he was a boy. She didn't share the part about how her heart had broken when he left. He hadn't said goodbye. It had broken her heart because she'd allowed herself to believe the fairy tales they'd spun as they'd ridden bikes and played in the creek. At thirteen she'd really believed that someday they would get married.

And like all young girls, she'd believed in their dreams of a perfect life and a happy home, where no one would ever yell or hurt them. Ever again.

She'd found happiness on this ranch. She felt

secure here. And she wondered if Carson was chasing after happiness, too, hoping to help his children feel secure in a life, a world, that had dealt them an incredibly difficult hand.

She looked down at the dark head of the boy in the swing and smiled. She could so easily get attached to him and to his sister. She could get attached to their father, too. She loved Jack like the father she'd never had, and she knew how badly he wanted to reconcile with his children. But she knew it would only be heartache for her if Carson and his children stayed for more than a day.

She glanced at the spot where Skip had been playing with a stick. The puppy and stick were both gone. She slowed the swing and scanned the area but didn't see a trace of the puppy.

Great. She'd gotten distracted and the Labrador had done what he most loved: wandered off. "Andy, keep swinging. I'm going to look behind the shed for Skip. Stay right here in case he comes back. He would be very sad if he came back and we were gone."

Andy nodded and he remained on the swing, his little legs kicking back and forth. The shed, a mere twenty feet away, was one of Skip's favorite places to hunt feral cats. She could hear his low, puppy growl. As she rounded the corner of the shed, he took off.

"Skip," she called out, knowing it would do no good. He would never make a good service dog if she couldn't break him of his need to chase cats.

She was coming back around the shed when she saw Carson and Maggie heading their way. He glanced at her and then looked around, his fatherly concern evident even from a distance.

"Where's Andy?" he asked as he got closer.

"On the swing," she answered. But he wasn't. "He was right there. I told him to wait."

Carson shook his head. "He walks away. I should have warned you. Hold Maggie and I'll find him."

"It's only been two minutes. He couldn't have gone far." She took Maggie and the little girl patted her shoulder and whispered, "Oh, Andy."

Kylie turned in circles, scanning the yard, the fields and the road. Where could Andy have gotten to so quickly? As she started her own search in the yard, Isaac walked out the back door of the house. She waved him down and he headed her way at a lope.

"What's up?" He pushed the brim of his cowboy hat back revealing just the edge of the scar that ran from his jaw to the place just above his left ear.

"Andy ran away from me. Two minutes and he was gone. If you get Max, he could help."

Isaac was already walking away. "I'll get him and a couple of the guys. We'll spread out in the field and head toward the pond. Kids always seem drawn to water."

"Thank you." The words came out choked as tears filled her eyes and clogged her throat.

"Don't mention it. And don't worry, we'll find him." With that Isaac took off, heading first to the kennel where Max barked as if he already knew he was needed.

Kylie shifted Maggie to her left side, giving her weaker right side a break. The toddler leaned her head on Kylie's shoulder and started to sing, "Jesus Loves Me."

"Yes, he does, sweetie," Kylie told her. "And he loves Andy. So we're going to pray real hard and we will find your brother."

They had to find him. Her heart ached, knowing that because of one moment of her distraction it could result in a child being lost. The thought cut deep because it brought back the accident. A distracted moment and their convoy had been attacked.

She'd lost so much that day.

She'd never expected that five years later she would be here. She'd thought her world would never be right again after that day. But she'd managed to save herself and she'd dragged Eric

Baker from a burning vehicle. He had proposed on the spot, telling her it was meant to be.

They'd known each other, had dated a few times, but he'd convinced her that her rescuing him that day had sealed their lives together. They'd lain there waiting for help, laughing at every stupid thing just to keep from crying.

Two months later they'd gotten married.

A year later he was gone and she was alone. Again.

Her heart thudded hard as she became frantic, worrying that she wouldn't find Andy. What if he'd gone toward the road or the pond? What if he wandered to the woods and darkness fell? She glanced toward the west at the sun that was barely a sliver of orange as it sank over the horizon. It would soon be dark.

"Maybe he went inside?" she said to Maggie, but she had fallen asleep in her arms. "Right, well, let's go check inside."

She headed for the patio and the back door of the house. As she hurried through the home she called his name. She checked the kitchen, the utility room, the garage. As she walked back through the dining room, Jack called out to her.

"What's going on?" he asked.

She didn't want to worry him. He'd already had one spell.

"Well?" he questioned as he reached for water, his arm and hand shaking uncontrollably.

She picked up the water glass and held it for him. "I lost Andy."

"You lost him?"

"One minute he was on the tree swing and the next minute he was gone. Isaac is getting Maximus and a few of the guys to help search."

"They'll find him." Jack reached. "Let me hold that sleeping princess. It might be the only chance I ever get to hold her."

Kylie placed the child in his arms. Maggie shifted a little, then settled back into a sound sleep.

"I knew I didn't have much of a chance of getting him to stay," Jack said as he studied his sleeping granddaughter. "I'll take the time I can get. You go help find Andy and the two of us will be just fine."

"If she wakes up?"

"Rosa is here. She's cleaning upstairs and she's going to make soup. We'll be just fine."

The housekeeper. Kylie had forgotten that Rosa planned on coming in for the evening because she would be gone over the weekend to attend one of her sons' weddings.

"I'll go help them look. You stay put." She leaned to hug Jack. "Don't worry. We'll find him."

He grinned. "I know you will. And in the

meantime, I get to spend time with sweet Maggie here."

Kylie gave him a last look and headed out the front door, just in case Andy had gone that way. The look on Jack's face had been priceless. She knew what this visit meant to him, even if it didn't go the way he'd planned.

She knew what this visit meant to her, too. It made her question everything she'd believed about her life here. She had spent four years finding herself, building a stable and happy life. For the first time, she had hope. She had real faith. She was truly happy.

And she didn't want anything to change, because change was unpredictable.

And what was more unpredictable than a man from the past with his two children showing up out of the blue?

Chapter Three

Carson had made a quick search around the stable, the corrals, the dog kennels. When he didn't find Andy, he headed back to the stable. Andy could very well be hiding in a stall or a storage room in the mammoth-sized facility. There were a dozen stalls, several storage rooms, an office and an attached indoor arena. Plenty of places for a little boy to hide.

Kids loved barns. Dusty barns with haylofts and dark corners to hide in. This wasn't one of those barns. It wasn't like the one that Carson and his siblings had played in when they'd been kids living here.

He didn't have time to think about the changes to the ranch. He had to find Andy before his son found trouble. It wasn't the first time he had wandered off. Their nanny had lost him twice in the past year. A friend had suggested a phone with a GPS tracking device.

"Andy? Andy? Are you in here?" He paused to listen for any sound that indicated his son might be hiding inside the stable. Nothing. He closed his eyes and felt the closest to praying he'd been in three years.

The night he'd lost Anna.

That night had been a night of prayer. Carson had determined God could and would get his wife through the trauma of the accident. And now, he was about to close his eyes and ask that same God to help him find his son.

He'd believed that his faith died the day Anna died. But if a person's first thought in crisis was to call on God, maybe he wasn't so far gone.

After a thorough search of the stable, including stalls where some pretty decent Quarter Horses pawed at the ground or snuffled water from automatic waterers, he exited on the opposite side. Isaac joined him, leading a big chocolate-brown Labrador Retriever.

"This is Maximus." Isaac patted the animal's head.

He led the dog in a circle, talking to him in a low tone that got the animal's attention.

"Does he know what he's doing?" Carson asked as the dog began to sniff the ground.

"Nah, but he'll do his best. I hope you don't

mind, I helped myself to this jacket in your SUV. I wanted him to have Andy's scent." Isaac held up Andy's jacket that had been left in his car seat. He adjusted his cowboy hat, exposing a military haircut and a scar on the left side of his head.

"We should keep moving. Is there still a pond past the stand of trees over there?" Carson nodded in the direction of the setting sun.

"Yeah, we'll head that way. Max seems to like that idea."

"How do we know he's on the right track?"

Isaac laughed a little. "We don't know, but I trust Max. I promise you, we're going to find your kid."

The way Carson saw it, he had no other options. He had to trust the dog and Isaac. Carson hoped that God realized he was putting some trust in Him, too.

"Kylie is really beating herself up," Isaac informed him as they continued in the direction of the pond.

"She shouldn't. Andy has done this before." Carson scanned the area and then shifted his focus to the horizon. "It'll be dark soon."

"I know. We have to keep moving. How often does he do this?"

"Twice in the past year. One time before that."

Carson hated the feeling of loss each time Andy wandered away. Loss and helplessness.

"There's got to be a way to stop him or to track him," Isaac offered.

"I've thought about several things. I guess I hoped he would grow out of it."

Max began to bark and started to pull on the leash.

"He's got the scent." Isaac unhooked his leash and the dog took off.

Max headed for a stand of trees a short distance from the pond. Isaac stumbled a bit. Carson passed him and went after the dog. His barking increased in frequency and loudness. Carson hurried to the pond bank where the dog seemed to have something or someone cornered. He prayed it would be his son.

He refused to think of other prayers that hadn't been answered.

"Andy. You have to come out." Carson stood, listening. Isaac approached, quieter than a man his size should have been.

"Over there." Isaac pointed to a huddled form sitting on the ground next to a bush, a tiny kitten in his hands.

"Hey, buddy, what do you have there?" Carson asked as he picked his son up.

"I saved it," Andy said. He leaned his head on Carson's shoulder.

Andy was a little muddy, wet and obviously cold. “Hey, Isaac, do you have that jacket?”

Isaac leaned down to pet Max, giving the dog a treat from his pocket. Carson repeated the request for the jacket. This time Isaac looked at him and then shook his head. Carson pointed to the jacket.

“Sorry, I didn’t hear you.” Isaac handed over the jacket with an easy grin. And Carson knew there had to be more to the excuse.

They headed back across the field. As they walked, Isaac texted Jack, Kylie and the men who were helping in the search. As he texted he moved to the opposite side of Carson. The side without a scar, Carson realized.

“Go easy on her,” Isaac said.

Carson knew he meant on Kylie. “I don’t need to be told what to do.”

“You don’t seem to be the most forgiving guy in the world.” Isaac grinned at him and then stuck a toothpick in his mouth. Carson could smell cinnamon.

“And you’ve come to that conclusion because I don’t want to take Jack up on his clinic offer? I’m a trauma surgeon, not a family practitioner. And I need to live in a larger city. I need to make sure we’re somewhere that Andy can get the resources he needs, the education he needs.”

Isaac’s expression softened as he looked at

Andy, clinging tightly to Carson's neck. "Yeah, I get that."

"Thanks."

Isaac shrugged. "It wouldn't hurt you to look at the clinic. And you could at least tell the old man that you forgive him."

"Yeah, I guess I could." Carson kept trudging along on the uneven ground. Isaac walked next to him, the toothpick between his teeth and a thoughtful expression on his face. It didn't take a genius to realize the other man looked a lot like family, more like Carson's younger brother Colt than Carson, but the resemblance was there.

So were memories of his parents fighting, shouting things that his younger self had tried to ignore.

"You really want to raise your kids up there?" Isaac asked.

"There or another city like Chicago. I've got to find a job in a city that offers what I'm looking for."

"Right, of course."

They were getting closer to the stable. Carson could see people moving, watching. "How many people live here on the ranch?"

Isaac took the toothpick out of his mouth. "Usually a dozen or more. I don't count them all. Jack likes to take in strays."

"Interesting hobby for a man who let his wife take his kids." Carson heard the edge to his voice and stopped there, because Andy had looked up at him, gray eyes troubled.

"You all just need to talk. But I guess that won't happen if you're leaving tonight."

Andy shook his head. "I don't want to leave."

"I know you don't," Carson responded.

"Give the kid a break. Let him get a good night's sleep. Does it matter if it's here or a hotel?" Isaac shook his head. "I thought I was stubborn. You keep making excuses about how you have to get on the road and get your kids settled. But you won't stop to think that maybe staying a night here could be the best thing for them."

Carson glanced up and saw Kylie a short distance away, listening and worrying her bottom lip. She'd done that even at thirteen.

"I'm sorry," she immediately said. Tears filled her eyes.

"You don't have to apologize. He sometimes wanders away. It happens. It's happened to me, and to his nanny in Dallas. We do the best we can to keep him safe."

Andy's arms went around Carson's neck, an unusual moment for the two of them. Andy was rarely affectionate. The kitten Andy had shoved between them wasn't quite as affectionate. He climbed away from them and jumped to the ground, running fast in the direction of the shed where the rest of the litter now played.

"Where's Maggie?" he asked as they walked through the gate that Isaac had opened.

"Asleep on your…on Jack's lap."

"Oh."

She put a cautious hand on Andy's arm. "I was worried about you, buddy."

"Sorry," he said without looking at her.

"We have stew and biscuits," Kylie said. "Would you all like to eat before you leave?"

Andy tried to get down from Carson's arms. "I don't want to. I don't like the car. I want to go home."

Home. Carson sighed. They no longer had a home. They had possessions in a storage facility. They had clothes in suitcases in the car.

He followed Kylie to the back door of the house. Inside they were greeted by a dozen people lined up in the kitchen preparing for dinner. This was Jack's life, his mission. Or was it a ministry? A group of people starting over. If anyone knew how to help veterans, it would be Jack.

"Well?" Kylie asked, smiling when she noticed where his attention had gone. "This is Mercy Ranch. You should at least take a little time and see what Jack has done with the place."

"I can see what he's done. It's a good thing." It was easy to admit. A man couldn't deny what was right in front of his face. The cosmetic changes to the ranch were obvious, but the people were the main reason for the ranch. He got that. He understood why this would mean something to Jack.

"It is a good thing." Kylie looked over the crowd of people and then her attention turned to Andy. "You should feed your children. There's plenty."

"We would like to eat," he said. With those words Andy relaxed in his arms. "I should get Andy cleaned up first. And let Jack know that he's safe."

They could spend the night. He could let his children rest. He could give Jack time and listen to his explanations.

It all sounded easy. It seemed like the best plan. But he knew that nothing was ever as simple as it seemed.

When Kylie had woken up that morning, it had been a typical Friday like any other day. Chores to do, dogs to train and the weekend to look forward to.

She was happy. Content. Her life here at the ranch was good and she didn't need anything more. She had a home here, friends, and a career she loved, as a therapist. A career born from the needs of the veterans on the ranch. How could one day, actually just a portion of one day, change everything? She had never expected to see Carson. She hadn't known that Jack offered him the clinic. Jack had talked about it, of course, but he'd laughed and said Carson would never agree to leave his high-powered job in Dallas for a family practice gig in Hope, Oklahoma.

Carson West was not the boy she had known twenty years ago. He was a man still grieving the loss of his wife. He was a father trying to raise two children alone. He was a surgeon on his way to a new job and a new beginning. Jack's children might have been gone twenty years, but Jack had kept track of them.

And as much as Kylie tried to pretend it was in the past, she'd held on to each morsel of information about the boy she'd once known.

Carson had changed. But hadn't they all? She definitely wasn't the girl she'd been all of those years ago. She smiled at the memory of her teen self. She'd been too skinny, often barefoot and always looking forward to leaving Hope. And now she couldn't imagine being anywhere else.

With the others occupied with dinner, she slipped away to check on Jack. She stopped at the door of the family room. Jack had fallen asleep. The gentle rise and fall of his chest assured her he was okay. Maggie lay curled in his arms, her head against his shoulder, her cheeks rosy from sleep.

Carson appeared at her side, a cleaned-up Andy at his side.

"He's going to be okay," he said with quiet assurance.

Of course the minute he'd said the words, the tears she'd been holding in managed to trickle down her cheeks. She brushed the dampness away, thinking he wouldn't want to see her crying.

Instead his shoulder brushed hers and he leaned closer, his breath warm as it ruffled the hair near her ear. "We'll stay tonight. I'll give Maggie and Andy a chance to rest. I'll be here to make sure Jack is okay. You don't have to take all of this on yourself."

How did he know her concern? She was so used to taking on the troubles of the people at the ranch, which included Jack. She worried a lot about him.

She closed her eyes, and leaned her head just a fraction so that it rested on his shoulder. Memories were so difficult because she knew how it had felt to lean on the shoulder of a boy. He'd always made her feel safe. Even then, when he was all arms and legs and not so tall.

The man standing next to her wasn't a boy. She took advantage of his strength, his nearness, just for a moment. Just long enough to feel strong on her own.

"We should get the kids something to eat," she said as she drew away from him.

Maggie blinked a few times, saw them and slid off the side of the recliner to toddle their way. Her mass of blond curls framed her sweet face and she smiled a sleepy smile. And then she walked right up to Kylie and held up her arms. Kylie lifted the little girl and held her close.

A tiny hand patted Kylie's cheek.

"Okay?" the little girl asked.

Kylie laughed and shed a few tears because of the sweetness of the gesture. "Yes, Maggie, I'm okay."

She could get so attached to this little girl with her giggles and sweet smile. And to Andy with his cautious looks and the sadness in his gray eyes. If one afternoon had proven dangerous, she could only imagine if they stayed longer.

"You found him," Jack said, his voice groggy.

"We found him," Carson said. "He took a bit of a roll in the mud but other than that, he's fine."

Jack studied his grandson. "Rose makes the best stew. That should warm him up and make him feel better. I guess you're heading out soon?"

"We'll stay the night."

Jack nodded. "Good. I have something I want to suggest."

"I think we're good," Carson said. "We both know where we stand. And I'm not interested in the clinic."

Jack waved a hand at his son. "I'm not talking about the clinic or what's between us. I'm talking about Andy. He needs a dog."

Kylie felt her heart drop, seriously drop. It ached as it plummeted. Jack had told her he had an idea. He hadn't mentioned a dog. She knew it made sense. But she also knew what else it meant. It meant time. Working together. Carson staying here in Oklahoma.

"I can get him a puppy once we find a home in Chicago. I know that kids need pets."

Jack waved his hand. "No. Not a pet. He needs a service dog."

Carson paused his denials. "A service dog?"

"We train them here at the ranch, for our wounded warriors and for others in need. Service dogs are expensive but we're pretty good at keeping the costs down so we can donate them to those in need."

"Then those dogs are for service members who need them. We don't want to take someone's dog," Carson insisted. But Kylie could tell he was thinking about it. Thinking about a dog for his son.

"A dog would keep him from wandering," Jack told him. "It would keep him safe."

Carson sat down, Andy still in his arms. "I get that. But we're leaving."

"If you stay, we could get him a dog." Jack raised his eyes and met Kylie's, pleading. "What do you think?"

She couldn't deny Jack. Her gaze shifted to Andy. She couldn't deny a child. "We could get him a dog."

"See," Jack said with a smile. "Kylie is in charge of our dogs."

Carson smiled at her. "I think Kylie is in charge of everything around here."

Jack laughed at that. "She is, but don't tell her. She'll start asking for a raise."

"We'll stay the night and discuss a dog later." Carson stood. "But right now, I have to feed Andy and Maggie."

Kylie followed him from the living room. "Do you need me to get anything from your car, or is there something I can do to help?"

"If you can sit upstairs with Andy and Maggie, I can get our bags. You don't need to carry them."

"I can sit with them," she offered.

He nodded and headed up the stairs. She had to hurry to catch up with him. Maggie clung to her neck and stairs weren't the easiest for her on the best of days.

"You could give me a break and slow down," she called out to his retreating back.

He stopped and headed back down the stairs. Before she could protest, he took Maggie so that he held a child on each hip. And then he tromped back up the stairs.

"Which door?"

"Second door on the right," she told him as she caught up. "It has a double bed and a twin with a trundle."

He opened it and entered the room. She watched as he set both kids down on the bed. "Stay with Kylie. I'll be right back with clean clothes."

"You've got this parenting thing down," she said as he brushed past her to leave.

Her words stopped him and she saw the change in his gray eyes. A soft smile played at the corners of his mouth. "Yeah, I've kind of had to figure it all out on my own."

She touched his arm, stopping him from walking away. "I'm so sorry."

"Don't." He paused there, just a breath of space between them. "I'd guess you have your own story. Life never turns out how we expect it to, does it?"

"No, it doesn't. And I think Jack isn't who you expected, is he? You thought you'd show up and everything would be the way it was when you left. You thought Jack would be the same person."

"Maybe," he said with a shrug of broad shoulders.

Time and circumstances had changed Carson the same way they had changed her. The boy she'd known had been fun-loving. In spite of his circumstance he had laughed and found the best in each day. The best in people. He seemed to have lost that side of himself.

The man standing in front of her had jagged edges.

Chapter Four

Carson woke up Saturday to the gray light of early morning stealing through the curtains of an unfamiliar room. Across the room in a twin bed, Andy and Maggie were cuddled together, still sleeping. From downstairs he could hear the sound of water running and dishes clinking. Sneaking from the room so as not to wake the children, he made his way downstairs.

If either of the children woke, he'd hear them or see them as they came down the stairs.

He had expected to see Kylie in the kitchen. Instead Isaac stood at the sink filling a coffee pot with water. He glanced at Carson, grinned, then went back to work.

"Expected someone prettier, did you?" Isaac poured the water in the coffeemaker. "She's working dogs. Want some breakfast? Or are you heading out early? Chicago is waiting."

"In a hurry to get rid of me?"

"I like the kids. You I could do without. I can do without your suspicious looks. I can do without your judgment. So can Jack. You haven't lived his life. Have you ever been to war? Have you ever wondered if the last shot you took…"

Isaac shook his head, raising a hand when Carson tried to tell him they didn't need to have this conversation.

Isaac poured himself a cup of coffee. "We have to talk about the fact that you think you know everything. But until you talk to people and find out their side, their experiences, you don't know them. And you don't know your father…"

Carson grabbed a cup from the cabinet and watched the coffee drip into the pot, ignoring the younger man that he assumed was his brother. He should just ask. As Isaac said, you don't know a person until you know their story.

"You're probably right. But I guess that goes both ways. You don't know my story, either." Carson met Isaac's gaze, held it for a minute.

"Shoot," Isaac said as he raised his cup.

"Shoot?"

"Go ahead. Tell me your story."

Carson shook his head. "Where's Jack?"

"Gone to town already. You can't keep a good man down." And he put emphasis on *good*.

Carson glanced out the window and saw Kylie heading toward the house. She was dressed in boots, jeans and a T-shirt. A dog followed along behind her. She was smiling, talking to the animal. For whatever reason, she made this place bearable.

"Is that why you're still here?" Isaac said, more of a teasing tone in his voice.

"No. I'm here because Jack had an angina attack last night and because I couldn't put Andy and Maggie back in the car after the long day of driving we had yesterday. They needed a chance to rest."

"Right. Of course." Isaac finished his coffee and put the cup in the dishwasher. "The past has a way of catching up with us. Now if you'll excuse me, Doc, I have work to do. If you're bored, you can always saddle up and help out. Do you remember how to ride a horse?"

"I remember how to ride a horse, but I have Andy and Maggie, if you remember. And I need to check on Jack."

The door opened and Kylie entered, looking from one to the other of them. She carried a basket of fall tomatoes and squash that she put on the counter before heading for the coffee.

"Are the two of you circling each other like old barn cats?" she asked as she grabbed a cup.

Isaac grinned at Carson as he headed for the

door. "Nah, only one of us remembers what a barn looks like. Carson is more of a domesticated house cat."

"If Kylie will watch the kids, I'll meet you out there in fifteen minutes."

"I didn't realize you'd be so easily triggered." Isaac laughed. "Do you even have boots?"

"I'm sure Jack has a pair I can fit into."

"Suit yourself." Isaac headed for the back door.

"Would you be able to watch Andy and Maggie for me?" Carson asked Kylie.

"I don't mind, but I do have work to do today. And we need to talk about Jack's suggestion of a service dog for Andy."

Her tone was cool, professional. It didn't match her. It didn't match the warmth of her expression, or the freckles that dusted her nose. It was for him, that cool, distant tone. It was meant to keep him at arm's length.

He should have appreciated the gesture. Instead it had him feeling as if he was missing something.

"What's your opinion on a service dog?" he asked.

"I did some research this morning. I think the idea has merit. A service dog for a child with autism can help with social settings and sleep patterns, can stop repetitive behaviors and can also keep him from wandering."

Impressive. She'd done her homework. He had thought he'd done everything possible to give his son the most opportunities, including this planned move to Chicago. But he hadn't considered a service dog.

"If I did this, would it take time to train the dog? Would we need to come back?"

"You would have to stay," she said as she pulled a carton of eggs out of the fridge.

He couldn't see her face but he knew the idea of them staying bothered her. He knew his reasons for wanting to leave, but her reasons for wanting them gone were a mystery.

"Stay. As in, for a day or two?"

"A few weeks." She began cracking eggs in a bowl. "Do you want an omelet?"

He watched as she worked. "Is it the idea of Jack giving us a dog that has you upset, or is it the idea of me staying?"

She looked up, guilt written across her face. "I'm sorry, I don't know what's wrong with me. I want Andy to have a dog. I think it would change his life."

"But you don't want me here," he said with as much of a smile as he could muster.

"I didn't say that. I didn't mean to even imply it."

But he got the impression it was exactly what she felt. But today he didn't feel like pushing for answers. If he pushed that meant going down a path he didn't plan to pursue.

"I can't stay here for a few weeks."

She dumped the eggs in a frying pan and glanced back over her shoulder. "I understand."

"But I do want Andy to have a dog. I'll figure this out. If you don't mind watching the kids, I'm heading out to join Isaac. I need to show him that I can still ride a horse."

"I'll watch the kids. You try not to break your leg." She grabbed a granola bar out of a basket. "You have to eat something."

"Have a little faith in me." He caught the granola bar Kylie tossed his way.

"I do have faith." She let the statement speak for itself.

He lifted his foot.

"Will Jack's boots fit me?"

"I think so. Or you can try the clothes closet. Every now and then a guy moves on and they'll leave stuff behind. We have clothes, boots, hats, just about everything." She opened the door at the side of the kitchen. "Laundry room and clothing. Help yourself."

She'd been right about finding what he needed. Boots, a hat, gloves. He walked back out a few minutes later and she gave him the once-over.

"Even if you can't ride a horse anymore, you look like you can."

"Thanks for the vote of confidence." He paused at the stove. "When Andy wakes up, don't be offended if he won't eat. He has sensory issues."

"I'll handle it."

"He might be upset when he wakes up." Carson thought it best she know everything. In response she put a hand around his arm and walked with him to the back door.

"Carson, I handle adults with PTSD. I think I can handle Andy. And I'll do it gently. I'll go upstairs and when he wakes up, I'll be there."

She would handle his son, he realized. She'd do it the same way she was handling him. Her touch lingered and for a moment their gazes connected. And then she seemed to realize it. She backed away, giving his arm a pat that was more motherly than anything else.

"I know you'll be fine with them," he said.

"I'll go up right now and check on them if that makes you feel better," she added.

Carson headed for the stable; the chocolate Lab that had followed Kylie chased after him but then ran back to the house to bark at the back door. He glanced back and saw that she no longer stood at the door. Fool that he was, he thought she might stand there and watch him walk away.

"She's not watching you walk away." Isaac came out of the barn wearing that same cheesy grin he'd been wearing since yesterday.

Carson saw behind the facade. He saw the occasional flicker of pain, sometimes a flash of anger. Isaac wasn't all smiles. Far from it.

"Do you ever take that thing off and wash it?" Carson asked as he stepped inside the stable.

"My hat?" Isaac looked disturbed by the question. He tapped the brim of the black cowboy hat. "Why would I wash it?"

"I meant that goofy grin you wear all the time."

Isaac laughed. "Who knew you'd be so funny? And who knew you'd be like every other man that landed here. Might as well get over it. We all fall a little in love with Kylie, and then we realize her heart isn't open for business. She loves everyone. But she doesn't fall in love with anyone."

"I'm not looking for love any more than she is," he reassured the other man. And then he noticed activity at a large metal shop a short distance away. "What are they doing over there?"

Isaac pulled a toothpick from his pocket and stuck it in his mouth. He pulled out another, wrapped in plastic, and offered it to Carson. "Cinnamon, you want one?"

"No, thanks."

"That's the crew heading to the Lakeside Retreat and Boat Dock. It's one of the projects we're working on. The place sat empty for ten years and Jack bought it to remodel. There's another crew that heads to town. Jack bought a few of the old stores and he's remodeling and offering free rent for a year if people will start businesses that could help the community."

"He's an optimist if he thinks he can turn this town around."

"He's giving people jobs," Isaac said, the toothpick in the corner of his mouth. "I guess it's more about faith. And if that's the case, I'm an optimist, too. The others are saddled up and ready to go."

"How many of us?"

"Four are riding. Matt is on an ATV. He doesn't care for animals too much."

They headed through the stable to a back door and a small corral. Two horses were saddled and tied to the fence. Two people were already on their horses and a third was outside the corral on a four-wheeler. He waved a prosthetic arm and grinned.

"Matt on the ATV." Isaac nodded in Matt's direction. "Jules is on the Appaloosa."

"Hi, Jules." Carson walked up to them. Jules extended a hand to shake his. She had burn scars down the side of her face.

"Tyler on the road," Isaac said as he mounted the horse tied near the gate. Carson shook hands with the younger man, and then he started for the gray that had obviously been left for him.

"You remember how to make that thing go, right?"

Carson untied the gray and ignored the question. As if it hadn't been years, he swung himself into the saddle and reined the horse in the direction of the men who were waiting. Unfortunately, the horse had other plans.

Carson barely had time to gather up the reins before the horse started to snort and raise its rump in a halfhearted attempt at bucking him off. He clamped his legs around the animal's middle and the horse gave a good buck, twisting as he did.

He soon became somewhat aware that the other men stopped to watch. He heard a few chuckles, then he clearly heard Isaac yell, "Ride 'em, cowboy!"

Carson held on, talking quietly as the horse began to settle beneath him. The quest to throw him from the saddle ended with a big shuddering shake that started at the horse's head and went all the way to its tail. After that, the animal took a few halting steps and began to walk.

"Was it entertaining for you?" he called back to Isaac.

Isaac rode up next to him, still laughing. "Yeah, but I honestly didn't think you'd be able to hold on. Spud is always kind of a beast when you first get on him."

"Payback," Carson warned him.

"Yeah, I reckon I'll get mine. I deserve that." Isaac glanced back at the house. "I was just trying to help you out. Kylie would have been all upset and tended to your wounds if you'd actually gotten thrown. I'm taking it the two of you knew each other, before."

"Yeah, we knew each other. How long have you known her?" Carson gave Isaac a quick look but he didn't quite trust the horse enough to let down his guard.

"Four years. Since she moved to the ranch. I know she lived down the road twenty years ago. That was a couple of years before my time."

Carson relaxed a bit in the saddle as he and the horse got used to each other. "How long have you been here?"

Isaac nudged his horse in to a trot. "Got here the first time about seventeen years ago. And I came back about five years ago."

The conversation fizzled as the men started

through a gate and rode toward a herd of cattle. It gave Carson something to think about. He felt as if his life, Jack's and Isaac's were all part of the same puzzle but with pieces missing. And Kylie belonged in there somewhere. He just wasn't sure what part she played.

He aimed to find out. And soon.

Kylie led Andy and Maggie down the stairs. They were dressed, hair brushed and ready for the day. Well, Andy's hair wasn't really brushed. The dark strands stood a little on end, but she'd done her best.

"Daddy is at work?" Andy asked, not looking at her as he did.

"No," Kylie assured him. "He went outside, but he'll be back soon. I'm going to fix you breakfast. Do you like biscuits?"

Maggie clapped her hands and jabbered about gravy, the words all running together. Andy bit down on his bottom lip and walked to the door.

"You have to stay inside, buddy," Kylie told him.

He nodded but she saw his hand fidgeting at his side, as if given a chance he would open the door and leave. The house phone rang and as she answered it she kept a close eye on Andy. She wouldn't lose him again. As she ended the call, she took the little boy by the hand and led him to the table. “Let’s sit right here, Andy.”

Maggie had already crawled up and sat down in another chair.

The door opened and Kylie’s roommate Eve Vincent entered, her gaze immediately going to the children. She waved a gloved hand at them.

“What’s for breakfast?” Eve stopped next to the children. “This must be Maggie and Andy. Wow, you can see the family resemblance. I saw their daddy getting on a horse earlier.”

Eve grinned. From the flicker of amusement in her eyes, Kylie didn’t have to ask which horse they’d given Carson.

“Please tell me it wasn’t Spud,” Kylie groaned as she dished out eggs, sausage and biscuits smeared with butter and jelly. She set a small plate in front of Andy and one in front of Maggie.

“Yeah, Spud. But he handled him fine.”

Andy shook his head no as he looked at the plate of food.

“Picky eater?” Eve asked.

“Sensory issues. The key is finding what food agrees with him.”

“Isn’t that just being picky?” Eve queried.

“No, there’s a difference. It’s about tasting food differently than you or I would.” She cut up the biscuit and Andy continued to shake his head. "What about the eggs?"

The little boy took a bite, made a face but continued to chew. Eve laughed at his reaction.

"I don't blame him. You're a good cook, Kylie, but eggs aren't your specialty."

"I make very good eggs," she countered.

"Hold on, I just remembered something," Eve said as she studied Andy. "Mind pouring me a cup of coffee and I'll help you get him to eat. I'm kind of a pro with kids."

"*You're* a pro with kids?" Kylie didn't mean to sound skeptical but her friend was either hiding something or making up skills she didn't possess.

They'd known each another for three years. Both of them were from completely different worlds. Eve had joined the military against her parents' wishes because she'd wanted some independence, and to prove herself. Kylie hadn't seen her mother since she'd been taken into foster care. After turning eighteen, the Army had seemed like the best option.

Eve now grinned as she spun her wheelchair around. "I'm sure I am a child expert. I've spent almost zero time with children, but look at me, I'm on wheels. That has to make a difference. Let me try to feed him something."

"Go for it."

Eve obviously thought she had a trick up her sleeve. She went to the fridge and pulled out taco sauce and ketchup.

"Watch and learn." Eve dropped the items in her lap and zoomed across the room at a reckless speed.

"What are you doing?"

Kylie followed her back to the table where Maggie had scooped the last of her eggs into her mouth. Andy was sitting in his chair staring out the window. Kylie peered over his shoulder and saw what had captured his attention. In the distance she could see the men on horseback riding herd on about fifty head of cattle, bringing them in to the corral to work them.

"Your daddy is riding. If we eat breakfast, we can go see him when they get back," Kylie said as she glanced at Eve who was busy separating Andy's eggs in to five piles. On the first she squeezed ketchup, on one she sprinkled sugar, the next pepper, one with taco sauce and the last with salt. This was her plan?

"There we go," Eve said, sticking her finger in the pepper and tasting. It made her sneeze.

Andy wouldn't try it but he laughed. When she tried the one with sugar his eyes widened and he tasted the sugar but not the eggs. When he got to the one with taco sauce he looked more than a little skeptical but after a taste he began to eat.

"Who would have guessed?" Kylie watched as the little boy ate the small portion of eggs and waited for Eve to wipe off the rest of the eggs and add taco sauce. "How did you come up with that?"

"I had a lot of time for reading while I lived at the rehab facility. After I finished up all of the books, I started on magazines. I have a lot of useless knowledge. Guess some that isn't quite so useless."

Andy finished eating all the eggs and he slid off the chair and headed to the door. "Hold up there, Andy. We have to all go together."

Kylie hurried to catch up to her young charge, scooping up Maggie as she did. She glanced back at the mess on the table.

Eve motioned to her. "Go on. I'll clean this up before I head back to the apartment."

"You don't want to go with us?" Kylie asked.

"No, I have to do some work." Eve had been a translator in the military. She now did contract work from home. She said it paid the bills and kept her out of trouble. And she didn't want to accept the help her parents offered.

Kylie and the kids left the house together. Kylie held Maggie's hand on her left and Andy's on her right, as they walked down the path to the stable. The men had returned. The cattle, some Hereford and some Angus, were milling about. The cattle dog, a border collie named Buster, circled through the herd, keeping them in a tight group. One of the men whistled and called the dog out of the corral.

Andy was enthralled. For that reason, Kylie didn't let go of his hand, even when he pulled away a little. She led him around the corral to the group of men who were dismounting. He saw his daddy and hurried forward, flinging himself at Carson. Carson lifted his son up and held him tight.

"Do you want to sit on the horse?" When Andy nodded, Carson sat the boy in the saddle and put the cowboy hat he wore on Andy's head. Andy grinned from ear to ear.

"Can I ride him?" he asked, speaking with more animation. She understood. Horses, dogs, all animals seemed to be great therapy for children and adults. They used a lot of animal therapy for the residents of Mercy Ranch.

Animals and plain old hard work.

Maggie reached out and Carson placed her in the saddle behind Andy. Kylie stretched her arm and rolled her shoulders. She'd never realized that one small child could be so heavy.

At one time she'd been strong. A roadside bomb had done more than broken her bones, it had robbed her of muscle strength. It had taken away her ability to have children. The injuries she'd suffered had left the surgeons no choice but to do a partial hysterectomy. So each time Maggie wrapped those sweet arms around her, each time Andy smiled up at her with one of his rare smiles, she felt happiness, anger, loss.

Carson being here with his children brought back more than memories of the past. She thought she'd dealt with everything, figured out the path her life would take and come to terms with what was lost and what she still had. Now, with their presence, a wave of longing swept over her, making her wish for things that could never be.

Life wasn't fair. It took things. Important things. But she knew how to survive. She knew how to find faith. She knew in time she would deal with how it felt to have Carson and his children on the ranch, small reminders of what she couldn't have. And she would somehow smile through this and survive.

Chapter Five

After giving the children a short ride around the corral, Carson lifted them down and led the horse inside to unsaddle him. Kylie had taken control of Andy and Maggie, and they watched the process of removing tack, brushing the horse and giving him a good portion of oats. It had been a while since Carson had lived this life and when he had, it hadn't been quite like this. The ranch as he'd known it had been neglected, the barn falling in, and Jack had been a strict task master.

The West children had learned to do things the right way. Now that he was older, Carson could give his dad credit for that. Jack had taught him to work hard.

Jack had changed. The ranch had changed. Carson's father met them in the yard as they were walking back to the house. He appeared stronger than he had the previous day but Carson saw the tight lines around his mouth, he also noticed tell-tale signs of Parkinson's. Jack West wasn't a healthy man. Carson guessed that was the reason for the sudden need to make amends with his children. Having children of his own, Carson got that. As a father, he couldn't imagine letting so many years separate him from Maggie and Andy.

"I thought you'd be back in that fancy SUV and heading north as fast as you could go," Jack said as he reached to tousle Andy's hair. "Hey there, cowboy. Are you having fun?"

Andy looked up at Jack and nodded, his gray eyes as big as saucers.

"I wanted to talk more about the service dog," Carson admitted. And he definitely had considered leaving. Early in the morning, when the house had been quiet and he'd been plagued by the gut feeling that if he stayed one day it would turn into three.

And each day they stayed would make it more difficult for his children when they left. It had been hard enough to leave Dallas, leaving everything familiar behind. They'd left the only home they'd ever known. They'd left friends, their longtime nanny, everything familiar. He didn't want to have to separate them from this place, from these people, as well.

"Kylie is the expert when it comes to the dogs." Jack smiled at the woman standing nearby.

"I do have a dog that I think will work well for Andy." She spoke softly as she looked down at the child who had hold of her hand. "I thought we might wait until tomorrow to make the introductions."

"Tomorrow?" Carson blurted out in surprise. "Why not today?"

She still held Andy's hand and Carson watched as his son studied their joined fingers. His small and slightly darker hand in Kylie's slightly larger, paler hand.

"I have meetings today, and this will give Andy a chance to feel relaxed here on the ranch before we start something new."

He understood and he was thankful that she seemed aware of what Andy needed. But it meant another day spent here, at the last place on earth he wanted to be.

"How about a trip to town for a milkshake and curly fries," Jack offered with a smile for the children and then to Carson. "I could show you the clinic?"

The offer of milkshakes immediately grabbed Maggie's attention who clapped her hands at the suggestion and even reached for Jack's hand.

Andy wasn't quite as sure. He looked at Kylie and earned one of her smiles.

"You'll have fun," Kylie assured him. "I have to work but you go have a shake. I like chocolate."

"We can bring you one," Carson found himself offering. He told himself he offered because it was the right things to do, and because she'd managed in twenty-four hours what few people ever did. She'd made a friend of his son.

"That would be nice."

She left them standing there, and Carson had to admit to feeling a little bit out of his element on the ranch, with her and with Jack. But if he truly thought about it, he wasn't. He'd been here before, standing outside a barn after a long day of hard work and hearing Jack announce they were heading to town for milkshakes and fries. Even if his sister, Daisy, had been in the house, they'd make sure to take her along.

He tried to think of anything similar that he shared with his own children, and he couldn't. The last few years he had been burning the candle at both ends. He'd worked long hours, then came home and tried to be both mom and dad to his two children. He'd had sleepless nights topped with more sleepless nights.

The busyness of their lives had left little time

for living their lives. He had missed out. Andy and Maggie had missed out.

"Come on, you're looking a little down in the mouth." Jack tossed him the truck keys. "You drive. I'm feeling a little shaky today."

"But you were up early and in town before the rest of us even had coffee." Carson picked Maggie up and deposited her in the back seat of the truck. "I have to go get the car seats for the kids."

"No problem. I need to make sure I have my medicine, anyway. I had to get to town early before the heat got too bad. They're rewiring the cabins at Lakeside Resort. I wanted to make sure a few other things were finished first."

It only took a few minutes, then they were heading to Hope, and to Mattie's Café. It was a five-minute drive but it took Carson back twenty years. The town hadn't changed much, other than getting a little older, a little more tired. The highway going through town had maintained a few businesses. A small sportsman's store with hunting and fishing equipment, the grocery store that had been around for fifty years, a local fast-food place and a pharmacy lined the main road. He slowed, taking in the familiar sights, and the not so familiar. A newer metal-sided building with a gravel parking lot sat in what had once been an empty lot. The sign at the edge of the drive read "Hope Medical Clinic."

He pretended not to see. Jack cleared his throat as they drove past. It was a bait Carson didn't plan on taking.

Once he turned down Shoreview Drive, things changed. Mattie's Café had once been a general store. It had the big windows, the inset door, all marks of a building nearing a century in age. Mattie had maintained the building, giving it new siding on the front facade and a new awning that covered the front porch.

Across the road from Mattie's were the old storefronts, businesses that had been boarded up and forgotten.

Today there were people working on the buildings, trying to bring them back to life, he guessed. Carson slowed to watch the progress. If a person could call it that. Some things were better left alone. He couldn't imagine trying to bring this old town back to life.

"Is it worth it?" he asked Jack.

"To the people who call this home? Yes, it is."

Carson nodded. "You're right. I'm sorry."

"You don't have to apologize. These projects are worth it. To the town, to the people who are finding employment and satisfaction in rebuilding something." Jack pointed to a man on a ladder leaned against the side of one store. "Cap is thirty-two and until a few months ago, he was homeless. He was in Afghanistan when he got the news that his pregnant wife had been killed in a hit-and-run. It nearly destroyed him. People have stories, some of those stories are pretty tough. They need someone who understands and is willing to give them a chance to rebuild their lives. I guess lives are a lot like this town. It might look like something you'd give up on, but look a little deeper and you'll find hope."

"Stories like yours?" Carson asked as he parked in front of Mattie's. He'd never thought about Jack's story. As a kid it had only been about what Jack did to them, not what had happened to Jack.

"My story's not worth retelling. What happened to me is a long time in the past. I've dealt with it and moved on. Now I can help these men and women do the same."

"I'm glad you're able to do this," Carson admitted.

Jack reached for the door but paused. "It's okay to have some good memories of this place, you know."

"I know it is." Carson hadn't expected it, but being here brought all those memories back. Learning to drive a tractor, hauling hay, breaking his first horse. "I'm not going to make excuses for the man I was, I just ask that you forgive me. I wanted to be more. I wanted the best for you all." Jack pushed the door open. "We all have our stories." Carson's opinion of Jack had been based on the memory of a thirteen-year-old boy who hadn't known anything about life—or his father's life.

"It would have been nice to know that twenty years ago," Carson told him as he pulled the keys out of the ignition.

Jack ran a trembling hand through thinning gray hair. "There were a lot of things I should have told you. I should have explained what went on in my head at the time. I should have explained why you had to leave, and also the agreement I had with your mother. I signed away my rights to you all because I thought you would be better off without me in your lives."

Carson was surprised at the admission, and only the realization that his own children were in the car kept him from saying things he might regret. "I don't know if that makes me relieved or more angry. Maybe you can explain what the two of you were thinking?"

"It's a complicated situation." Jack took his hand off the door handle and brushed it across his face. "Your mother and I had more of an arrangement than a marriage. When she decided to leave, I had to give her full custody. I agreed to stay away. Then I regretted it. But the papers were already signed and I knew you all would be better off without me. But I was there. Even when you didn't see me, I was there."

Carson shook his head at a revelation that didn't make sense. Now wasn't the time to delve further into whatever crazy plan his parents had concocted. He didn't want to have the conversation with Maggie and Andy in the car. And he didn't want to hear more of what was starting to sound like excuses to him.

He got out of the truck and opened the back door to unfasten Maggie from her car seat. He glanced at Andy and saw that his son had already unbuckled his seat. "Good job, Andy."

The three of them met Jack on the sidewalk in front of the café. It was lunchtime so the place looked packed. Jack walked in ahead of them, his feet shuffling the slightest bit. A waitress called out for them to pick any place and she'd be with them in a minute.

A couple of farmers at a nearby table sat back in their chairs and stared. One of them finally nodded a greeting.

"Jack, is that your boy Carson?"

Jack's face split in a grin. "Yes, it is. And these young'uns are my grandkids. Maggie and Andy, that ornery feller is Gus Pipkin and his buddy is Carl Larsen."

"Who knew you'd have such good-looking

grandkids," Gus teased. He had a gray beard with streaks of red and hair down to the middle of his back. His cowboy hat was bent like it had been stepped on a few too many times.

Carson remembered both men. Gus had trained horses and Carl worked on the railroad.

The waitress appeared, looking a little bit frazzled. Her short gray hair was damp from perspiration and she had a streak of ink on her cheek.

"Got something right there, Rena." Jack pointed on his cheek where she had the ink spot.

"Thanks, Jack. Is this your boy Carson and his two little ones?"

"It sure is. We're here for milkshakes and curly fries. Oh, and when we leave, we need a chocolate shake for Kylie. Make that four. Can't take one of those girls a shake and not the others."

"We'll get that right out. But what about lunch?" Rena pulled up a chair from an empty table and sat. "My dogs are killing me."

"You have dogs?" Maggie asked, wide-eyed.

Rena smiled. "I mean my feet. Do you like dogs?"

"Kylie's getting us a dog." Maggie chattered on about it, and Andy listened but didn't look up.

"That's pretty great," Rena told Carson's

daughter. "You know what—I'm going to get you all some sliders to go with those fries. Grandpa Jack forgets to eat sometimes and I have to remind him."

"Go on, now, Rena. You know I don't forget anything." Jack winked at her. "When was the last time I forgot your birthday?"

"Every single year, you old coot. But you always make it up to me."

With that Rena got up and hurried back to the kitchen, and Carson wondered at the relationship between his dad and the waitress.

Being in Hope brought back a tidal wave of memories for Carson. It was a bit like being an amnesiac who suddenly remembered who he was. And he wasn't sure yet if he liked what he remembered.

Because on the way to the café they'd passed the creek where he and Kylie had gone swimming that last summer he lived here. And he remembered telling her he'd marry her someday.

He hadn't kept the promise. Worse than that, until now, he hadn't remembered. He wondered if she thought about that day, about the dreams they'd shared and the plans they'd made.

Kylie sat across from three veterans who suffered from PTSD. One of the men, Donnie, also had some serious anger issues to go along with the diagnosis. She thought some of the anger had been with him for a lifetime, childhood trauma he hadn't dealt with. The PTSD compounded things for him and all of that was made worse by drug use. Frankly, he frightened her. And there wasn't much she was afraid of.

Maximus the chocolate Labrador retriever lay at her feet. Craig spoke, sharing a moment he'd had earlier in the week, and the dog perked up, watching, alert to the tone of his voice.

"Matt, what are some of the techniques you've used this week?"

"Music, the lavender." Matt shrugged. "I'll be honest—I'm doing a lot of praying."

"There's nothing wrong with that." She included them all in the statement. "Prayer, refocusing our thoughts, those are steps we can utilize. It's easy to focus on the memories, and then thoughts spiral out of control." She glanced at her watch, surprised by how quickly time got away from her. She'd already met with Eve, Miriam and Jules. And she still had to handle the dog situation for Andy. "We're almost out of time. See you all next Tuesday. Same time?"

"I can tell you something," Donnie interrupted.

"Okay, Donnie. Go ahead."

"I'm not okay with all of the prayer talk.

And I don't like lavender. I'm about done with this nonsense."

Craig leaned back in his chair, his fist clenching at his side. The last thing she wanted or needed was a fight between the men.

"I'm sorry you feel that way." She stood as she said it. The best thing would be to have the three men walk away, in separate directions.

Matt stood but didn't walk away. He got right up to Donnie and looked him straight in the eye.

"Donnie, I don't care what you like or don't like. I'm going to survive. I'm going to live my life in peace. And if I pray, that's no business of yours. If you decide you want help, you let us know. But next week, don't show up at this session."

Donnie made a noise that was a cross between a snarl and a laugh. "And you and your one good arm are going to do what to me, little man."

"And that's the end of this." She put a hand on Matt's arm and moved him toward the door. "Let's go. There's work to do."

"I don't feel like working today." Donnie ground the words out. "I'm going to town."

They all stepped back as Donnie charged from the room. They followed at a slower pace.

"He's using again," Craig stated as they left

the house. "Jack needs to order a urinalysis on him."

"I'll tell him." She watched Donnie walking down the road because he didn't have a car.

"I think it's time for Donnie to relocate," Matt said, his hand going to Kylie's back in protective mode. "You okay?"

"I'm good, worried, but good."

"Watch out for him, okay?"

"I will. And thank you." And then she saw Carson.

He carried a bag and a tray with four cups. Milkshakes. The idea of a chocolate shake made her unbelievably happy. Just the chocolate shake, she told herself, not the man standing on the sidewalk looking for all the world like he still belonged here, as if he hadn't left years ago and just come back for a for a short stay in their lives.

The children were playing with Jack. She watched as they hurried toward the swing. Jack followed at a slower pace, less steady on his feet than he'd been six months ago.

"Is Jack okay?" Matt asked.

"He's good. Just needs to rest up after yesterday."

"Isaac is worried about him."

"Yeah, we all are." She smiled at Matt. "I'm going to check on him. Need anything else?"

"Nope, I'm good. One arm and all. I hope Donnie knows that I have a lot of strength in this one arm."

"I'm sure he doesn't, but as long as you know your own strength, inside and out, you're good."

"Thanks, Kylie. And I hope you know, you do make a difference here."

Matt walked away, and when she turned around, Carson was right there. His eyes looked lighter today, more silver than gray. He was watching Matt.

"I could use some chocolate right about now," she said as she took one of the shakes. "I take it those are for Eve, Miriam and Jules."

"Jack said for the four girls I'm assuming he meant you ladies."

"He did. I'll take these inside."

"You okay?" he asked as she started to walk away.

"I am. Why do you ask?"

He cocked his head to the side and studied her. She was struck by the sweetness of that look and how much it reminded her of him as a boy. Except he wasn't a boy anymore. He was a man. A man who had loved, married, lost a wife and was still hurting. She could see it in his eyes.

"I'm not sure about that," he told her. "First, you all came out of the house after a raging bull had already escaped. And he looked bent on destruction. Second, you're limping. Did he hurt you?"

"No, he didn't touch me. Donnie is always angry but we're working on that."

"You didn't answer my question about limping."

"I'm okay. It has to do with one leg being shorter than the other, lacking some muscle, throwing everything off. It's like putting one tire that is different from the others on a car."

"Nice analogy. I'll use that sometime if you don't mind."

He glanced beyond her shoulder and she did a quick check to see what he was looking at. Donnie. Her pulse quickened a bit but she told herself she didn't have to fear him. Yes, he was angry, but not with her.

"I'll walk with you," Carson offered.

"I can take care of myself."

"I know you can. But I'm offering to walk with you." He opened the brown paper bag and offered her a French fry. "I'll bribe you if I have to."

"That really isn't fair. I can't say no to curly fries."

He grinned. "I know you can't."

Of course he knew. She smiled at the memory of him bringing lunch to their secret meeting spot down at the creek. Jack would take him to town to the diner, and he'd always bring extra back for her. Jack must have known because since the day she came to the ranch, brokenhearted and hurting, he would bring her chocolate shakes and fries.

"Your dad knew," she told Carson.

"What?"

"About the shakes and fries that you would bring me," she said as she reached for another fry in the bag.

"Oh, yes. I always asked if we could order extra for you."

The memory meant more than before, because she knew that both father and son had been looking out for her, a poor kid from the trailer park. She wondered if Carson knew the role his dad had played in her life.

"He called child protective services." She sipped the milkshake. "Did you know that? A month after you left, a caseworker showed up at our house. They took one look at the situation and loaded me up in a car. I never went back. I never saw my mom again."

Silence. He looked troubled. They had reached the apartment door. She put her hand on his arm. "Carson, it changed my life. For the better. I went to a foster home with a lovely older couple, and then I joined the military."

"I'm glad. I'd told him that I worried about you. But the night we left, I didn't have time to say anything, to care about anything other than keeping my brother and sister from falling apart."

"It's fine, Carson. I understand. We were just kids." She shook her head, remembering the stories they had shared with one another.

"Yes, we were kids."

"We survived," she said.

He touched her hair, sliding a strand behind her ear. His eyes became molten silver as he studied her face, his gaze lingering on her lips. She wanted him to kiss her. But she knew they couldn't. Shouldn't.

He knew it, too, because he stepped back. "Yes, we survived. And we haven't stopped surviving. For a long time I felt like I was just existing, getting through each day, hanging on to get through another day. But it gets easier. I wanted to be angry with people when they first told me that. It made me angry. How dare they tell me that I would get over losing my wife?"

She closed her eyes at the truth in his words, the pain.

"But it does get easier," Kylie agreed.

"There are days I feel guilty for that. But then there are the other days when I know that's what I'm supposed to do. We're supposed to heal. The body, the heart, the emotions… We're made to survive, to heal, to knit ourselves back together. Sometimes there are scars, but we heal."

"Oh, Carson." She put a hand to her eyes that were welling up with tears, wishing he hadn't said those words, not that way.

He touched her cheek, his hand strong, gentle.

"I have to take these inside."

"I know."

She stepped away from him, needing a break from the upheaval of emotions he'd caused. She didn't want to walk away. She wanted to stay near him, near his scent, which was spice and outdoors. She wanted his arms around her, which was a dangerous thought.

She thought about healing and wondered if that's where she was at in her life. She'd worked so hard on herself, on realizing happiness had to come from within. She didn't want to lose sight of that.

But it had been a very long time since she'd wanted to be held, since she'd considered being loved. It was both a strange feeling—and a good one.

Chapter Six

The distant sound of church bells and the nearer sound of children laughing woke Carson from a sound sleep. It had taken him a minute to remember where he was. When he did remember, he jumped up, unsure of the day or time. Andy and Maggie were not in their bed. That made sense. He'd definitely heard laughter. How long had it been since he'd woken up to a house filled with laughter?

How had Jack managed to keep them here for more than a week? Part of it was that Kylie had yet to decide on the right dog for Andy. She'd introduced a couple but neither was a good fit. She said it wasn't something to rush into. He suspected Jack was orchestrating the delays.

Carson had complained, albeit half-heartedly. He hadn't expected to stay. He had a job interview that had been postponed. But he also knew that this place, the brief visit, had been good for Andy and for Maggie.

When he'd stopped here at the ranch, he hadn't expected to find Andy, the little boy who smiled and talked, hiding within the quiet, pragmatic little boy he'd been raising for the past three years.

He couldn't leave now. Not yet. Because he had to stay and see how the dog would work out for his son. That meant everything to him. It meant more than his anger with his father. It meant more than his fear that his children might get attached and make leaving more difficult.

And Kylie. Every time she looked at his children, he saw heartbreak in her eyes. He knew that leaving wouldn't just be difficult for Maggie and Andy.

Laughter rang out again.

Curious, he made his way down to the family room, found it empty, then followed the laughter to the kitchen. Kylie smiled as he entered the room; her gaze dropped to the floor and at her feet he could see Andy and the puppy Skip. Maggie sat nearby playing with a doll. Carson paused to take in the moment. The most normal moment he'd witnessed in a very long time.

He watched as the puppy pounced again, trying to get something Andy had in his hand. After a moment the animal gave up and plopped on the floor, resting his head on his paws. Andy grinned and pulled his hand out from under his leg and started to move it back and forth. Skip jumped at his hand and Andy said, “No!” The puppy sat down. Whatever Andy had in his hand, he now gave to the puppy, laughing when his hand got licked in the process.

This was the normal he’d been searching for. The normal he hadn’t been able to create. Their nanny Mrs. Wilkerson had loved his children very much, but even her cookies, her hugs, hadn’t changed things in any real way.

As he stood there contemplating things, Maggie saw him and with a screech got to her feet and ran in his direction. He picked her up, and she gave him a quick hug and kiss on the cheek.

“Daddy.” She leaned her head on his shoulder.

“Maggie May.” He kissed her forehead. She giggled.

“Good morning, sleepyhead.” Kylie greeted him as she stirred eggs in a bowl and then poured them in the frying pan.

“I never sleep late,” he defended. His eyes narrowed as she reached for taco sauce and sprinkled it in the pan of eggs.

She glanced his way. “You should. At least every now and then. I’ve heard from doctors that sleep is important for good health.”

"You've got me there," he agreed. "What are you doing to the eggs?"

She grinned. "Well, I'm adding taco sauce. My friend Eve started this yesterday. She put several different things on Andy's eggs. Sugar, salt, pepper and taco sauce. He liked the taco sauce best."

"I don't know what to say. But if it worked, I'll buy cases of taco sauce."

Maggie squirmed to be free of him. He set her down on her feet and she made a beeline for Kylie, who smiled down at her. Then Maggie wrapped her arms around Kylie's legs and hugged them tight.

"I love you, Kylie." Maggie held tight, then toddled off to retrieve her doll.

Carson didn't know what to say. Kylie's back was to him and he didn't think it would be for the best if she turned around to look at him. Not at that moment.

His children were getting attached to Kylie. But whatever they felt here, it had to be temporary. Temporary, like the moments he and Kylie had shared as young teens. Caught up in the sweet mystery of young love, figuring out how to feel so much for someone and still be your own person.

Whatever he felt for the woman standing there with bare feet, hair in a ponytail and a little flour on her cheek was just leftover emotions from junior high.

Kylie flipped the omelet. “Your dad called. He wanted to make sure you all planned on going to church with us.”

Church? He hadn’t been… He took a sip of coffee and watched as Kylie flipped the eggs again.

“Where is my father?”

“He had to go check on Gus. He said Gus called this morning and didn’t sound like himself. So your dad called an ambulance. They think Gus had a mild stroke.”

“I don’t know if we have time to get ready for church,” he said, then glanced at his watch. It was only eight in the morning? It had felt later than that.

“The kids are all ready to go. I’m ready to go.”

He stepped closer. “Actually, you have a little something right here.”

He grabbed a towel and wiped the flour from her cheek. And it felt too much like flirting, something he hadn’t done since—he counted back—since he and Anna had dated. It had been almost eight years since he’d flirted with anyone other than his wife.

Kylie’s eyes widened and she moved, quickly

brushing off his touch. She wiped her face with her hand "It's just flour."

"I know."

"The kids are excited about church. There's a puppet show today in the children's church."

"Kylie, we haven't been to church in ages. I can't..."

"Because of Anna."

It must have been something on his face. She blinked a few times, surprised.

"Am I not supposed to say her name?" she asked.

"Of course you can. I just..."

"You don't?" She reached for the towel, turned down the burner on the stove and looked at him with real interest. "Do you talk to the children about their mother? Show them pictures of her? Carson, she meant everything to you. You need to raise her children knowing that they had a mother who loved them and that you loved her."

"This isn't the conversation I expected." And he realized it hurt, yet it broke something loose inside him.

"I'm sure you didn't. But here it is, open dialogue. I'm not going to tiptoe around her name. I'll even tell you about Eric, my husband. He was a friend and we decided to get married because I thought I could fix him. I'm no longer in the man-fixing business, except here on the ranch."

"Ouch."

She laughed a little. "We're not so different, except that I'm honest with my feelings. Show them pictures, Carson. Andy can handle it. Maggie will jabber and not really have a clue but soon she'll understand."

"Thank you." He kissed her floury cheek. "I have to admit, most people still avoid talking about her."

"Because you look so wounded when they do. But I think you're better than you even know you are."

"Maybe."

"So we're going to church," she repeated. "And you need to get ready. I mean, if you really don't want to go, no one is going to force you. But think of it this way, it's another thing you've avoided since her passing. Would Anna really have wanted her children raised without church?"

He didn't know what to say. She reached up, smoothed his hair, then she touched his cheek. "I know you loved her. She must have been amazing. And I know you're always going to miss her. But you made this move to start fresh. So do it."

"Spoken like a true friend," Jack said, coming in from the utility room. "Sorry, didn't mean to interrupt."

"Of course you didn't." Kylie grabbed a coffee cup and poured Jack a cup. "Breakfast is ready, Jack."

"Don't mind if I do. Carson, get those kids a plate. Let's get this show on the road. When we get home, we can introduce Andy to his dog."

Carson grabbed a couple of plates and scooped out eggs, biscuits and sausage for Maggie and Andy. Kylie had poured them each a glass of orange juice. Even though the kitchen was large, they brushed past each another a couple of times. It was a comfortable situation. Maybe more comfortable because of her straightforward conversation with him. She knew where he stood but he didn't really know where she stood.

She was very good at deflecting, making the conversation about the other person. And never talking about herself.

He'd picked up the plate when he noticed Jack sitting at the dining room table. His face was pale and beaded with perspiration. The bottle of nitro pills was spilled across the table.

"Kylie, call 911." He tossed the plates on the counter. "Get the kids out of here."

He picked up one of the pills and tried to get it in Jack's mouth. "Jack, open your mouth. Now."

Jack opened his eyes but shook his head.

"Don't argue with me! I came here to set things straight and we haven't had a good conversation yet. You have things to tell me. Remember?" He managed to get Jack's mouth open and he got a pill under his tongue.

Behind him, Maggie was crying and Andy made humming noises. Carson pulled his father to the floor. "Kylie, can you take the kids to Eve?"

"Give me a minute." She stood next to him, the phone in her hand. She spoke to the dispatcher, giving information about Jack's condition.

"Get me the blood pressure monitor. Tell them I'm a doctor."

She nodded, hurrying to Jack's chair. He could hear her rummaging in the drawer. A minute later she returned. Jack gave her a weak smile but then his eyes closed.

"Kylie, the kids."

"Yes, I'm taking them. I'm going to get Isaac."

He nodded. He wasn't going to argue with her. Isaac probably should be there. Eventually they'd have to discuss how the younger man fit into this situation, and into their family. Obviously this wasn't the time. He watched as Kylie left, his children in tow. Jack's blood pressure had dropped dangerously low. That was to be expected after administering the nitro pill. But he was nowhere near out of the woods. The door opened and Isaac appeared, his hat in his hand.

"Heart attack?" Isaac asked as he stepped close, his hand on Jack's shoulder.

Carson nodded. "The ambulance is on the way."

He wrapped the blood pressure cuff around Jack's arm.

"I'm going to pray," Isaac told him. He said it with determined look.

"I'm not going to stop you." Carson checked the blood pressure, loosened the cuff and bowed his head.

And as he prayed, he prayed for faith. Because he hadn't had any in a long time.

Sirens wailed in the distance. The door opened. Kylie appeared. Carson's breathing eased as she knelt next to him, taking his hand.

Kylie stood in the hallway outside Jack's hospital room. She could hear Carson inside talking to his dad. He heard Carson tell him this was an unfair way to get him to stay in town longer. Jack said something and the two laughed. Isaac was in there, grumbling about people with no sense of humor.

Kylie stepped into the room, needing to see

for herself that Jack would be okay. She'd given the three men time alone. Now it was her turn.

Isaac and Carson both stood up. She smiled at the display of manners, as much a part of them as their gruff exteriors and gray eyes. She edged closer to the bed and Jack opened his eyes and half grinned.

"Now don't look so gloomy. I'm fine." His voice was weak and raspy.

"No, actually you're not. You had a heart attack."

He patted her hand where she held the rail of his hospital bed.

"Kylie, you know I'm too mean to die. I'll be home in a day or two."

"Do you think so?" Carson asked.

"Well, I plan on it," Jack quipped.

Carson pointed to his chair. "Have a seat, Kylie."

She sat next to Jack and watched as he reached for water, his arm trembling from the shoulder to the tips of his fingers. Carson picked up the cup and helped Jack sit up.

"Slowly," Carson warned.

After taking a drink, Jack leaned back. "I'm going to tell you boys something. I'm tired. And I'm going to need help getting things ready for the fall fishing season."

"Why are we worrying about fall fishing?" Carson asked.

"Jack's trying to bring tourism back to Hope," Isaac answered. He remained seated, his legs stretched in front of him, his hat low over his eyes. "Arts and crafts, a fishing tournament and live music."

"I'm sure you have plenty of people to make sure it gets done," Carson told him. "That's not something you need to worry about right now."

Jack sighed. "While you're here, you can help out. Isaac has most of it handled. But I really need to find a doctor for Hope. If you know of any doctors who'd be interested? Or if you could do the interviews..."

"I'm not going to be here that long. Jack, I have a job interview in Chicago. I've put it off for a week, but I can't put it off forever. We have all of our personal possessions in storage waiting to be moved. Maggie and Andy need to be settled somewhere."

"I know, I know. I just thought that while you're here helping Andy with his dog..."

"I'll do what I can. But I can't stay for a month. I'm sorry."

Jack nodded. "I understand. Have you called Colt and Daisy?"

Kylie looked up and met Carson's troubled gaze.

"I called them."

"I guess they don't care." Jack hesitated. "I don't blame them. But I'd like for them to know the truth. I told your mother I'm not hiding it any longer. I'm too old."

"Hiding what any longer?"

Kylie started to get up but Carson shook his head. His expression, the look in his eyes, said he wanted her there. *Needed* her. She didn't want that. She didn't want anyone to need her that much. Ever again.

She didn't want to let anyone down.

"Jack?" Carson prodded him, touching Jack's arm. Then he looked at the heart monitor.

"Leave him alone," Isaac said. He came to his feet but reached for the wall to steady himself. "Let him rest."

Jack shook his head, his face pale against the blue of the hospital pillow. "I want to say this. If something happens, she won't tell you. Stubborn. I needed her. Your mother. She was my nurse in the hospital after I came back from Nam. I knew that if I came back to the ranch alone, I'd blow it. I made a deal with her, to marry me. We planned on staying married for ten years, long enough for me to get my act together, and then she'd go and I'd give her a settlement. I thought it would be easier than it turned out to be. And then there were kids, so she stayed longer and we tried. But in the end, she couldn't stay. She couldn't keep you all there. She got the money I had promised her from the beginning, and she got you kids."

The long confession took all of his strength and he closed his eyes.

"*That's* why you stayed away?" Carson stared at the man in the bed as if he couldn't quite understand what he'd just been told.

Jack opened his eyes again. "I didn't stay away. But we'll talk about that another time."

Kylie reached for Carson's hand, needing to stop their pain. "We should go and let him sleep."

"Isaac?" Carson asked.

"I'm right here."

"Yes, you are. And I'm assuming you're my brother?"

Jack gave a weak nod. "I cheated on your mother."

It was too much. Kylie could see Jack growing weaker, even if his sons couldn't. They were too focused on untying the knots of their past. And what difference did it all make now? It was the past.

Kylie stood and leaned over Jack. "Sleep now. We'll be back tomorrow to check on you."

"You take care of them and don't let them use their fists on each other. Stubborn."

"Must be genetic. So are you." She kissed his forehead. "I love you, Jack."

"You know I love you, too."

Kylie led Carson from the room. Isaac took another minute and then he joined them. For a moment she thought he planned on punching Carson. Instead he shook his head and started down the hall to the elevators.

"I can't even..." Carson said. "How in the world did two adults make such a mess out of their lives?"

"People make mistakes," she defended. "Eric and I got married because we were friends and we were both wounded and alone. It was crazy and impulsive. I regret it, but I don't."

She took that back. In his mind, in his heart, Eric had been very alone.

"What happened with the two of you?" Carson asked, pulling her over to the side.

She watched as Isaac stepped on the elevator. The door dinged. He pushed it back open and gave the two of them a long look. And then he shook his head and let the doors slide closed.

"My husband killed himself."

He crushed her to him, holding her close, her head tucked beneath his chin. Safe. She felt so safe in his arms. She wanted to pretend it wasn't real. She didn't want to get used to the feeling, to him.

He led her to a small room with vending machines and instant coffee. A lady poured herself a cup of coffee, gave them a terse smile and left.

"What happened?" he asked her, when they were finally alone.

"His pain levels were off the charts and he got addicted to pain medication. When they started cutting him back on the pain meds he found heroin. He was depressed, addicted and in pain. And I was in the hospital having surgery."

She hadn't been there for him. She had loved him; he'd been one of her best friends, and she'd failed him.

"I wasn't there for him," she said again.

He looked away, but not before she saw the pain that flickered in his gray eyes.

"I'm so sorry," he said. "I am sorry for everything you've been through."

"You don't have to be sorry," Kylie whispered. "I'm still breathing. I'm making it through every day. I'm not a broken person, Carson. Don't think that you have to rescue me."

"I know you're strong. And you rescue everyone else." He touched his forehead to hers, and she wanted him to kiss her.

She was strong, but she needed to know she was still a woman. Still whole. When his lips finally touched hers, it was sweet. Disarmingly sweet. He held her gently as if she might break.

But she wouldn't. She'd been refined by fire. She'd been through the hardest things a person could go through and she was still standing.

Chapter Seven

Ten days. That's how long Carson had been on the ranch. It was the most time he'd taken off in a few years. Thirty-two months to be exact. He exhaled, letting go of the frustration and various other emotions that still unsettled him. Guilt. That one wouldn't go away. Guilt because Anna was gone but she should be here with their children.

Frustration because they should have been in Chicago. But he couldn't leave with Jack still in the hospital.

Worry because each day his children got a little more attached to this place and to the people who lived here. Each day he spent with Kylie, he remembered what it felt like to enjoy someone's company.

He ran a brush down the neck of the horse he'd been working with that morning, the same horse he'd tried to convince Jack was too wild-eyed. And the animal had been wild-eyed until Maggie had taken an interest. Who knew a toddler singing "Jesus Loves Me" could change an animal's entire demeanor?

He smiled at his daughter. She was sitting a short distance away brushing her doll's hair, oblivious to the big, red coated horse that had dropped his head to watch. The gelding's ear's twitched and he seemed to sigh.

"What's going on here?" Kylie asked as she walked down the center aisle of the stable, slid past the horse and stopped next to Maggie.

"Maggie is taming the savage beast," Isaac said as he came out of the office. "Look at that horse."

Carson grinned at his daughter. "Keep singing, honey. Maybe he'll let me clean his hooves."

Isaac arched a brow at that. "You know how to clean hooves?"

"I wasn't always a surgeon."

"Don't ruin those million-dollar hands of yours," Isaac teased. He handed over a pick. "I rode him pretty hard yesterday."

"And you don't groom your horse before you put him in the stall?"

Isaac turned a little red. "He might have thrown me."

Carson tried to bite back the laughter but he failed. "You should have had Maggie sing to him."

"I wish I had known her skills." Isaac rubbed the top of Maggie's head, tousling her blond curls. She gave him a pert little look and went back to singing.

Carson stood close to Red's side and faced his back end. He eased his hand down the horse's front leg and found that Red wasn't really opposed to having his hoof lifted for a good cleaning. He finished one hoof and went to the next side.

When he finished, Carson tossed the pick back to Isaac.

"Ready to meet Andy's dog?" Kylie asked. "I think we've finally settled on the right one for him."

Carson had been ready for a week. "Sounds like a good idea."

Isaac snorted. "No, you go ahead. I'll be here when the buyer gets here." He shot Kylie a questioning look. "Which dog?"

Kylie gave Isaac what had to be a warning look. "Rambo."

"But he's…"

She cut Isaac off. "He's the perfect dog for Andy."

Isaac shook his head and walked off.

"What was that all about?" Carson asked as they walked across the lawn toward the apartment Kylie shared with the other women.

"I don't know what you mean," she said as she kept walking. "Andy already met Rambo. He is a big fan."

"Where's Andy, and the dog. Rambo?" Carson asked, and he wondered if he would get used to calling a dog such a ridiculous name. "Couldn't you have named him Buddy? Or Sam. Something other than Rambo?"

At the question, Kylie laughed.

"Andy is with Eve. You have something against Rambo?" she asked.

"Not really. I'm just afraid that every time I speak for the dog, I'm going to do it in a Sylvester Stallone voice."

"If you do, I want to hear it." Kylie hefted Maggie to her hip but not without a grimace of pain. He reached for his daughter.

"Let me carry her."

Kylie shook her head. "Nope. I've got this."

He agreed; she had this. And she had him, in a way that took him by surprise. It was only temporary, he kept telling himself. For himself and for Maggie and Andy. He'd promised Anna that he would always make the best choices for his children. And for Andy, that meant a city with resources for education, medical and other special services their son would need.

He could have stayed in Dallas but he had needed a change. He needed a home where he didn't have memories of Anna everywhere he looked. Memories of her in the kitchen. Memories of her on the porch swing. Memories of that last day when she'd needed milk from the store. Milk. Just a gallon of milk. That was the memory that he couldn't escape. He wanted to remember the good memories, but constantly being reminded of that awful day, he needed to escape.

A change meant moving on. Not just for himself, but for the children. If he didn't let go, they couldn't let go.

"I talked to Jack today," he told Kylie as they walked.

"So did I." She chuckled. "He sounded much better. You know he isn't going to stay in the hospital and have all of those tests they want him to have done."

"He has to. Kylie, he probably needs open heart surgery."

"They've told him that before. He wouldn't do it. He was afraid."

"Of course he's afraid. That's understandable."

She shook her head. "No, afraid something

would happen and he wouldn't be able to tell you all how sorry he was for everything that happened."

"Maybe now that he's told me, he might have his surgery."

She allowed him to take Maggie from her and he immediately set his daughter on her feet and took her by the hand. "She can walk, you know."

"I know, but I don't mind carrying her."

"She's getting too heavy to carry." He slowed his pace for his daughter. Maggie had other ideas though. She stopped to pick dandelions and she handed them to Kylie.

The door of the apartment opened and Eve exited with Andy next to her. Andy started to walk away. Eve stopped him, redirecting him in Maggie's direction. He sat down on the grass next to his little sister, and the puppy, Skip, joined them. "What happened when you and your siblings left here?"

He stood next to her watching his children. "We went to Texas and our mother got a job at a hospital. She met a guy that made Jack look like a saint. On the outside he looked great. He treated her well. But he wasn't interested in having children around." He cleared his throat and she saw the way his hands clenched at his sides. "Good man. Took us to church. And he knew how to use a belt in a way that would have surprised most people. As soon as we could, we all left home. When Daisy turned seventeen she moved in with me. Colt moved to a ranch with friends. He's a bullfighter for the pro bull-riding circuit."

"Daisy?"

"She has a boutique in Tulsa. But I have a feeling you knew that. Jack seems to know a lot about our lives."

"He does. But he needs to tell you more." She leaned against him. "It isn't so bad, is it?"

"What isn't so bad?"

She laughed. "This talking business. With your dad. About the past."

He hadn't shared, not the most important stuff. But Kylie thought he had. He'd kept the worst parts to himself. And she'd given him everything. Every single broken part of herself.

He thought it would be easy to love her. Isaac had told him that everyone at the ranch fell in love with Kylie. Of course they did. And it made him angry with all of those men who thought they loved her.

It made him wish he was a better man. A man who wouldn't send his wife, nine-months pregnant, alone to the store. He would never forgive himself for telling her that he couldn't go. And he would never be able to tell anyone that if he hadn't been so busy, she would still be alive.

Suddenly she cleared her throat. "Carson. You okay?"

"Of course," he assured her. "Just thinking. This dog, he's how old?"

"Three. And that isn't what you were thinking about."

"Close enough. And he's a trained service dog."

"Yes, of course. He's worked with people who have PTSD and also physical limitations."

"How did Andy react to him?"

"Amazing. They bonded immediately. You know I introduced him to Maximus, but the two didn't have this same chemistry."

"This is going to be a change for us. We've never had a pet before."

"And that's why you need to train yourself. This is a pet, but he isn't. He's a part of the family, but he's more of a caregiver."

He watched her as she spoke, as she explained the role of Andy's new dog. The sun danced across her face and he could smell the warm scent of her perfume mixing with the coconut scent of her shampoo. She studied him with golden hazel eyes.

"Carson, focus."

He grinned and laughed a little. Caught in the act.

"I'm focused. I'm focused."

She needed someone better than him. But he wanted to be the only man in her life. And that told him he had lost his grasp on reality.

Kylie cleared her throat and stepped back. The children and Eve were a short distance away. And being distracted by Carson West was the last thing she needed. "Eve is waiting for us. And I'm sure the kids would like lunch." She backed away from him, from temptation.

Maggie picked a few more dandelions, counting each one as she added it to her bouquet. "This is for Eve." The little girl leaned down to pick a white clover.

She stood up with a shriek and started to cry. With tears streaking down her cheeks, she held her arms out to Kylie. Kylie lifted her.

"What happened, sweetie?"

"It bit me," she said, then Maggie cried more.

Carson gently took her finger in his hand. "A bee sting. We need to get something on that."

"We have something in our apartment." Kylie hurried toward her apartment. Carson and Andy followed.

She punched in the code on the alarm keypad, opened the door and yelled, "Man on board."

He followed, shaking his head.

"What?" she asked.

“I’m not sure if I should question the alarm system or the call to arms.”

“It wasn’t a call to arms. There are four of us, and no one wants to be surprised by a man in the house. And we have security because, well, it’s security. Not everyone can be trusted. You know that.”

No women appeared, but a loud bark greeted them. Andy hurried forward without hesitation, wrapping his arm around the dog. Kylie carried Maggie to the kitchen where she rummaged in the cabinet for a medicine that promised to remove stingers. Carson took it from her, told her it might not work and asked for her credit card.

Kylie grabbed her purse off the counter and produced a debit card. “Sorry, no credit cards. Are you going to hit the ATM?”

“No, and this will work just fine.”

“You don’t want tweezers?” she asked.

At the word *tweezer*, Maggie sobbed and wiped at her face. “No tweezers.”

Carson dropped a kiss on the top of her head. “No tweezers. They squeeze and we don’t want that.”

He took the card from Kylie and gently scraped until the stinger worked free of the skin. Kylie handed him a bag of ice wrapped in a paper towel.

“All better?” he asked.

Maggie shook her head, her brown eyes overflowing with tears. Tears that melted Kylie and made her want to give the child anything. Carson held her for a moment, stroking her blond hair back from her face. She sniffled a few times, then reached for Kylie. Eve appeared, Andy following.

"Uh-oh, we have tears. Andy and I picked all of the dandelions and then we thought we should check on his little sister. How is she?" she asked.

"She's all better," Kylie answered, smiling at Maggie as she said it. Her heart ached because moments ago the little girl had reached for her, wrapping those small arms around Kylie's neck and making her wish for things she couldn't have. A child.

Carson's child.

And for his two children, he would do anything. Even put aside his plan for vengeance against his father. If he'd truly planned vengeance. At the very least, he'd come to tell Jack what he thought of him.

And God had had other plans. That's what she thought. God's plan included healing this family. Eve had made her way down the hall and she returned with Rambo. Part of the plan. The dog immediately went to Andy, sitting obediently at his side.

Kylie made eye contact with her friend, noting the hint of sadness but acceptance with the plan. Rambo had been a part of their lives since they'd taken him in as a puppy. But letting go was made easier when they could see what a difference the animal would make in the life of a child.

With Maggie starting to calm down, Carson moved across the room to watch Andy. He sat at the dining room table, giving the boy and his dog space. Maggie leaned in to him and quietly called, "Come here, puppy."

Rambo's tail thumped the tile floor but he remained at Andy's side. With a hand gesture from Eve, the dog plopped to his belly.

"Carson and Maggie, this is Rambo. Eve trained him and he's the best." Kylie made the introductions and she ignored the questioning look Eve shot her. That look accused Kylie of being less than honest. And she wasn't dishonest. Eve did a lot of work with the dogs. That included Rambo.

Kylie lowered herself to the floor and sat next to Andy. She held a hand out to Rambo and the dog gave it a lick. She watched to see if Andy would follow her example. He did.

"Rambo likes to go for walks," she told the child. "But only if you hold his leash. Remember what I told you, you have to always hold his leash. And if he stops, that is his way of telling you to stop. That means you can't go, because Rambo says it isn't safe."

She smiled at the little boy and he smiled back.

"You understand, right?" Kylie asked. "Because only big boys get dogs like Rambo. You have to take care of him."

"I'll take care of him." Andy spoke softly.

"I know you will," she assured him. "Do you want to walk with him? I'll go with you."

"What has Rambo been trained for?" Carson asked.

"He's multipurpose," Kylie answered.

"He picks things up for me," Eve offered. "He's also very comforting."

Carson eyed the dog and didn't look completely sold on the idea. "Aren't Labs pretty hyper? They like to run."

"I understand your skepticism, but when trained properly, Labrador retrievers put work first. They put their person first."

"Show me," Carson said.

Eve spoke the dog's name and Rambo was all attention. He sat next to her, his focus on her and not the two children who had been rubbing his ears and face. "Rambo, lights."

Eve pointed. Rambo trotted across the room to the light switch and pushed up on the switch.

He returned to Eve's side. She pulled the glove off her hand and dropped it.

"Pick it up."

Rambo obliged. She gave him a loving pat and Kylie saw the glimmer of tears in her green eyes. Eve wasn't a big woman. She was five feet nothing, less than one hundred pounds. She was small but mighty and had the heart of a giant. She understood why Rambo would be best for a child. But they both knew how much it would hurt to give him up.

Kylie caught a movement from the corner of her eye. Carson had moved; his gaze connected with hers and then he studied Eve. He was too observant.

"Eve, is Rambo your dog?" he asked, his gaze shifting from her to Kylie. He caught her shaking her head no. She widened her eyes, going for innocent.

He sighed and his gaze dropped to his son. Andy had a treat in his hand, a small dog bone that Eve must have given him. Kylie felt sorry for Carson. He appeared to have the weight of the world on his shoulders. Yes, they were broad shoulders, but still, it couldn't be easy. Now, in addition to worrying about his children, and Jack, he would worry about taking their dog. She didn't want that to be an issue.

They trained dogs for this purpose, to pass them on to others.

Eve glanced her way before answering. "He's our dog. All of ours. He does a multitude of things in this home. He knows when someone is sad. He can pick things up for us. He turns on lights. He's an all-around good dog."

"We can't take your dog. I appreciate the offer, Kylie, but this dog belongs to you, to the women who live here."

She ignored him. Andy had moved close and his little hand rested on her shoulder as she sat on the floor next to him.

"Andy, why don't you call Rambo? Say *Rambo, here.*" She held her hand for the dog to stay where he stood.

Andy shook his head.

"You don't have to. But if you did, he would go for a walk with you."

Andy bit down on his bottom lip, his eyes shifting from the floor to the dog. Ah, he was thinking about it. He smiled a little.

"Rambo, here." His voice was quiet, tentative, sweet. The dog immediately moved to his side.

"Take his harness, like this." She showed him how to hold the dog. "And of course you can always hug him."

All of the other commands had been just words to the little boy. When she told him he could hug the dog, he closed his arms around Rambo's neck and held on. The dog whined a little as he moved to put his head on Andy's shoulder.

Kylie started to push herself up but Carson's hand was there. She took the offer of help and smiled up at him. "Thank you. I think we should take Andy outside and show him that some things are off-limits."

"How will he know?" Carson asked.

"Rambo has lived with four women. He's stubborn. But there's something else he can do. We've been working with him on this."

"What's that?"

"When Andy uses repetitive motions, Rambo will stop him. We had a girl who used to pick at her skin until she bled. We trained him to distract her. Distraction is a wonderful way to retrain someone."

His hand still held hers. Distraction. She could give a long speech on the many ways it could be used to a person's advantage. She blinked, paying attention to the child and his dog.

"Eve, do you want to come with us?" Kylie asked as they walked out the door.

"No, thanks." Eve gave Rambo a last pat on the head, but then her gaze lifted to meet Carson's. "I think I'll stay in here out of the way.

But I want you to know that we made this decision together. We love Rambo but we know he can do the most good with Andy."

Carson inclined his head, then he reached to shake Eve's hand. "I appreciate that."

"Where do you want to take Rambo?" Kylie asked Andy.

"The horses," Andy answered, his look solemn. He held the harness and Rambo stood quietly at his side, ready for his command.

"Okay, you lead."

Andy led and they all followed.

"Do you see the difference?" Kylie asked Carson as they left the apartment.

"He's more confident." Carson's tone held wonder. "I should have thought of this."

She was taken aback by the comment. "You can't think of everything."

"I know, but..."

"Did you ever stop to think that God had a greater plan for your trip to Hope? You're here and it seems like one thing after another is stopping you from leaving. And I know you don't want to be here. But look at Andy and think about that."

"You're right."

She fell back, putting her hand to her heart. "I'm right?"

"You're right."

Andy had reached the fence with the horses, and Kylie held Carson back. Andy tried to go through the fence and Rambo wouldn't budge. When the child tried to let go of the halter and crawl through, the dog moved to block him.

"That's amazing," Carson said.

"Yes, it is."

"Thank you," Carson said. His lips brushed her hair as he spoke.

Andy returned to their side with his dog. Rambo sat and Maggie wanted down to pet him.

"You have a best friend," Kylie said. The words came out watery as she fought the tears that threatened to spill out. She wasn't prone to waterworks but Andy and Maggie seemed to bring out that side of her nature.

Andy needed a best friend. The kind of friend Rambo would be to him. Loyal. Always willing to be loved and to love back.

She thought his daddy needed one, too. Maybe if he had a friend he wouldn't look so alone most of the time. But it wasn't her place to think about Carson and what he needed or didn't need. He was an adult. He could take care of himself.

For all she knew, he did have a friend, someone he counted on. She didn't need to be his person.

That was actually the very last thing she needed.

Chapter Eight

On Wednesday Carson left Maggie and Andy with Eve, because she'd taken the task of teaching them to work with Rambo. He thought it was easier for her than Kylie, because Kylie was too attached. Both to the dog and to his children. He headed for the corral and Matt met him there.

In the nearly two weeks he'd been on the ranch, he'd grown to like Matt. He respected him. Matt had lost his left arm when an IED exploded as he drove through a town in Afghanistan. After his multiple hospital stays, he'd tried to go home but he'd found that he no longer fit in there. He'd heard about Mercy Ranch, and a year ago had moved to Oklahoma.

"So what's the plan for today?" Carson asked the other man.

Matt nodded toward the men in the arena. "Riding lessons."

"Riding lessons?" He hadn't expected that.

Matt grinned and ran his hand through shaggy blond hair. "More like therapy. But a lot of these guys can't ride. Not only have they never been on a horse, but with their physical disabilities riding is more of a challenge. If they can't get on the horse, they walk it, brush it, spend time with it."

"What can I do to help?"

"We have a couple of new guys. They need help saddling their animals, and then we'll leave it up to them how much they want to do with the horse."

Carson headed for the men who had horses tied to the outside of the barn with the lean-to shading them. One of the guys greeted him. The man next to him was too busy working on his saddle.

"Need help?" Carson asked.

The man standing next to the big paint horse turned. Carson realized he wasn't a man. He was a kid. Twenty years old at the most. He had a scar along the right side of his face and his right arm appeared to be paralyzed. But he smiled.

"Dude, that would be great." He stepped

back. “I’ve never been on a horse and I don’t have a clue how to saddle him.”

Carson lifted the saddle pad first, eased it into place, then settled the saddle on the horse’s back.

“Next the girth strap.” Carson stood on the horse’s left side and reached for the strap that hung on the opposite side. He pulled it under the horse’s belly and through the ring. The kid standing next to him watched intently.

“What’s your name?”

“Joe.”

“Well, Joe, your horse is saddled.” Carson handed him the reins. “I’m not sure what they’ll want you to do now.”

“I guess I’m going to ride this bad boy.”

“It’s a girl,” Carson pointed out, and Joe laughed.

“So you’re Jack’s other son?” he asked.

“Yeah, I am.”

“Is he okay?”

Carson patted the kid on the arm. “He will be.”

His phone rang. He recognized the Chicago number. “I have to take this.”

“Sure, no problem. Thanks, Doc.”

Carson walked away, answering the phone as he did. “Dr. Carson West.”

The person on the other end greeted him, then

let him know that he would have to be in Chicago in the next week if he wanted to interview for the job. He thanked them and told them he would try to be there. He pulled a pen and paper out of his pocket and wrote down the number, repeating it back.

He hung up, then noticed Kylie standing behind him.

"I didn't want to interfere," she said.

"No, of course not."

"Job interview?" she asked, looking disappointed.

"Yeah. They're giving me another week, but then they have to pick someone. I get that."

"I'd hoped you would be here for Jack's surgery. But if you can't, that's understandable. We'll get Andy used to Rambo..." Her voice trailed off.

"If I don't go, the job won't be there." He realized that the job in Chicago no longer seemed like the most important thing. He'd gotten sidetracked here. By the ranch, by Jack, by the woman standing next to him. Kylie.

Kylie cleared her throat, gaining his attention. "We have church tonight and there's a potluck. If you want to go. I just wanted to let you know. I didn't want you to wonder where everyone had gone to."

"We'll go."

"Oh, okay." She seemed surprised. "How was your visit with your dad yesterday?"

He'd taken Maggie and Andy to see Jack at the hospital.

"It was good. He told me he's going to keep thinking of ways to keep us here. I told him I can't keep putting off the inevitable."

"He will try. I guess it won't work though, will it?"

"No, it won't work." He glanced past her, at Matt and the others, already saddling their horses. Therapy. He realized the horses had been doing that for him since he arrived. It felt good to be here, to connect with this part of his past. "A year ago I realized we were living our lives as if we still expected her to come home. Or maybe I was the one living that way. Maggie and Andy were existing with a father who wasn't really there for them. We need this change. I realized in the past year that we have to move on, keep living."

"You don't have to convince me," Kylie told him, her voice sweet, soft.

He knew he didn't have to convince anyone. Other than himself.

The conversation ended and they ended up side by side, watching as Joe and the other men worked with their horses. Joe had only managed to lead his horse. He looked uncomfortable even though the mare plodded along docilely.

"I'm going to help Joe."

"I'll watch from here."

As Carson approached, Joe stopped. The horse also came to a standstill. "Want to ride?"

Joe looked up at the horse. "I think for now I just want to lead him."

"If you change your mind, let me know."

"Sure thing, Doc." Joe saluted.

Carson returned to Kylie's side. She was watching the men but he could tell she was distracted. She pushed a stray hair back from her face.

"Have you started over?" she asked.

Her question shifted pieces of him, emotionally, physically. A year ago he would have told her that starting over wasn't an option. He was living his life as best he could. That had changed when he realized that the act of just getting through each day wasn't helping his children.

"I'm making an attempt."

"That's a start." She glanced toward the house as a truck rolled up to the garage. "I know how it feels, Carson. I know that feeling of being so shattered by something that you wonder if you'll ever find all of the pieces of yourself. I've heard all of the platitudes. People say they understand.

And they say it'll get easier. You want to scream at them that it isn't getting easier. When will it get easier?"

He searched for words that he hadn't expected to need. "And then one day you realize you got through twenty-four hours without crying. Another day passes and you realize you laughed for the first time in a long time."

"Yes, that's it. It's called *moving on*. What a sanitized word for something so difficult." She touched his hand with hers.

It didn't take much for him to come to the realization that he was indeed moving on. And that he was enjoying the company of the woman who had once been a childhood sweetheart. He hadn't expected that. He'd been numb for so long, now was a really awkward time to suddenly notice a woman.

He was a surgeon; he knew how this worked. When circulation was returned to a limb that had been deprived or cut off from blood flow or oxygen, it started to feel things it hadn't felt in a long time. Life returned.

She released his hand. "Oh, you've got to be kidding me. I'm not sure how Jack talked Isaac into bringing him home. Isaac is usually pretty good at handling him."

He didn't know at first what she was talking

about. Then he realized Isaac had a passenger in his truck.

"We should go see what they're up to." Kylie glanced back to see if he was following her.

"I think that's probably a good idea."

The two of them hurried toward the house.

"Don't try to run," Carson called out.

Jack had a hand on the door and he paused, ever so slightly. "I'm not running—I'm just ready to sit in my recliner and give people orders."

"You're going back to the hospital is what you're doing." Carson walked up behind his dad, noticing that Jack's legs shook and his breathing was labored.

"I'm not going back. They want to cut me open." He headed inside, not giving Carson a chance to stop him. Not that he would have. Jack obviously needed that recliner.

"Maybe they want to cut you open because it's the best way to keep you alive. Did you ever think of that?" He put a hand on Jack's arm. Isaac had the other. "You'll have to do it eventually."

Jack made his way slowly to the family room and the big leather recliner. "I missed this chair. Hospital beds are torture devices."

"Did you do the tests?" Carson asked.

"Yeah, I did a few. And then I told them I'm done. I wanted to be home. I was afraid you would leave without saying goodbye."

"I wouldn't leave without saying goodbye. And I think you know that."

"You don't seem to listen," Jack whispered.

Isaac loomed, leaning against the wall next to the chair. Carson glared at him. "Why don't you sit down?"

"I guess because I don't want to." The other man just grinned, chewing on a toothpick that hung from one corner of his mouth. And then he touched a finger to the brim of his cowboy hat, adding a bit more to the challenge.

Carson took a step in his direction, really wanting to forget he wasn't a man of violence. "First, do no harm." Yeah, he remembered the Hippocratic Oath.

"Stop. Both of you." Jack shot Isaac a look. "Go sit down."

"Yeah, brother, why don't you go sit down?" Carson shot a look at Isaac that didn't faze him a bit. But the whole situation made Carson wonder what he'd done with his better self. Obviously packed up and sitting in a Dallas storage unit.

"I'm not going to sit down because I don't like being told what to do," Isaac said without a bit of anger. "And you don't like to be challenged.

I guess you're used to being the big boss. And around here..."

Kylie touched Carson's arm. He glanced down at her, somehow forgetting her presence. He shouldn't have forgotten. No doubt it was all the male saber rattling that had caused his memory lapse.

"Let's focus on Jack," she said, sweetly but meaningfully.

"That's what I'm trying to do. He needs to go back to the hospital."

"I said, I'm not going back," Jack growled. "Isaac isn't the only one who doesn't like to be told what to do. I'm a grown man. When I'm ready for open heart surgery, I'll let you all know."

"The fact that you seem to think you have a choice is what amazes me. When a doctor recommends that surgery, he isn't saying that you might want to consider it. He's telling you that you need it. In order to live." He shot Isaac a look. "And you should be the one encouraging him to do what's best for his health and not the one driving him away from the only help he's going to get."

"Right, because he's going to listen to me."

"He has to listen to someone." He gave his full attention to Jack, his father. This was not the reason he'd come here—to get in the middle of Jack's medical situation, to argue with a man who was his brother and to find himself gaping at the woman he'd only known as a gangly girl with bare feet and the prettiest eyes he'd ever seen.

He should have left that first night. Better yet, he should have just kept on driving east on the interstate rather than taking that turn toward Grand Lake and Hope, Oklahoma. If he had listened to his wiser self, he would be almost to Chicago by now.

Instead he'd crash-landed in his past, but it didn't look anything like what he'd remembered.

That was both good and bad.

Kylie had no desire to be the referee in the Western version of Family Feud. Isaac, always a little angry, glared at Carson. Jack, pale and shaky, closed his eyes and seemed to be ignoring his sons.

Carson stared at his father, concern furrowing his brow. "Chest pains?"

Jack opened his eyes. "Pains, but not in the chest. The three of you. That's my pain. I'm seventy years old, so I think I can decide what I want to do about my health. I talked to the doctor. The two of us agreed that I can wait. Not long, but a few weeks won't kill me."

"I'd like for you to have the surgery in Tulsa," Carson informed his father.

Kylie figured telling Jack what to do was a little bit like trying to pull a mule where a mule didn't want to go.

"My doctor and I already made that decision. *Without* your help."

Isaac moved away from the wall, straightened his hat and gave Carson a look that wasn't hard to interpret. She'd known Isaac long enough to know when he was sending a message that a person's opinions weren't wanted or needed. Kylie guessed that meant Carson and Isaac weren't going to be best friends any time soon.

"Where are you going?" Jack asked as Isaac took a few steps.

"I've got work to do." Isaac stepped around the chair, shoulder checked Carson and kept on going.

Kylie stared after him, unsure of what to say or do. Isaac had some bitterness but he usually tried to get along with people on the ranch. Obviously Carson didn't qualify.

"Get back here," Jack growled.

Isaac stopped but he didn't turn.

Jack pushed Carson's hand off his wrist. "Oh, stop doing that. My heart is still beating. The two of you have to accept that you're brothers and neither of you is at fault for that. I'm to blame. I was about the orneriest man walking. You were there, Carson. You lived through it for thirteen years. I was an alcoholic, addicted to pain pills and on top of that, I wasn't very nice."

"You definitely had your moments," Carson said dryly.

Jack looked from Isaac to Carson. Kylie wished Carson would listen. Really listen to Jack. She knew that some apologies were just words with no meaning behind them. But with Jack, the proof was in the man he was today.

"Surprise, I'm your brother." Isaac tipped his hat at Carson.

"Yeah, definitely a surprise." Carson stood there, frozen; his gaze shifted from Isaac to Jack. It shouldn't be a surprise. After all, he'd noticed the family resemblance and had suspected this from the beginning. "And the family reunion has been fun. I'm only sorry it couldn't last a little longer."

"You and me both." Isaac said it with a smug grin.

It didn't take a therapist to know that these two men, Isaac and Carson, weren't going to hug it out. They both had too much going on inside them.

Isaac wore his anger like a badge. His mother had raised him until he turned ten, then she'd dumped him at Mercy Ranch. That's when Jack really started to get his act together, the way he told it. His wife and three kids had been gone a few years and he suddenly had another son depending on him.

Isaac didn't have warm fuzzy feelings about that time of his life.

Carson's attention returned to Jack, who immediately dropped his hand from his chest.

"Leaving the hospital was a bad decision. I'm not going to say it again. If you decide to go back, I'll be happy take you."

"I'm not going back. Not today. They'll arrange my surgery for next month, after the fishing tournament. I'll be fine until then."

"I hope that's the case. Right now I need to go check on Maggie and Andy."

Jack sighed. "Carson, I am sorry. I'm going to give you some advice. Forgive. And maybe pray for peace. You've been through a lot, but there is still good in the world. You have two beautiful kids that are proof of that fact."

"Thank you for the advice. And as for my children, I know what I have. Andy and Maggie are everything to me." With that, he left.

"That went better than I expected," Jack stated simply.

Kylie turned her attention back to him, studying his expression to make sure she wasn't missing anything. He was putting on a good act, but she could see the exhaustion in his face, the way he sank into the recliner. Isaac noticed as well, and he moved a little closer to the chair as if he intended to do or say something.

"Go on, take care of the horses." Jack waved Isaac on.

Isaac paused, unsure. He might act like he hated the world, but she knew he loved Jack. Jack had dragged him home from a VA hospital in Tulsa and put him back together with horses, sunshine and a mission: to make the ranch a haven for other wounded warriors.

"I know you can make your own decisions," Isaac said, his voice a little gruffer than normal. "But I don't want you to..."

"Oh go on, now. I'm going to be just fine."

"I know you are." Isaac looked away. "But I want you to know..."

"That you're going to make a champion cutting horse out of that gelding you just bought," Jack went on, in typical Jack fashion that Kylie both loved and hated.

Isaac cleared his throat. "That isn't what I was going to say."

"It's all I want to hear you say. Get out of here before I get up out of this chair and give you what for," Jack growled. Isaac grinned, tugged the brim of his hat and left, the back door banging on his exit.

"You do everything in your power to push them away," Kylie accused, knowing she had the right of it.

"Oh, I'm not trying to run them off. I just want to sleep." Jack pushed the control button on his recliner and the headrest went back as the footstool went up. "Ah, that's one hundred percent better than the hospital bed. And the food is a mite better."

"A mite?" she asked.

"Okay, quite a bit better. Although they did have good chocolate cake. Now, back to business. Is the dog helping Andy?"

"I think so. I've been doing research and it's going to do more for him than just keep him from wandering."

Jack nodded, his eyes closing. "You go on and do whatever you need. I'll be fine right here. I need to catch up on sleep. You know it's hard to sleep in the hospital with all that poking and prodding."

"I know."

He fell asleep almost immediately, so after a few minutes Kylie left him alone. As she crossed the lawn, she heard adult voices and children laughing. She rounded the corner of the women's apartment and saw Carson, Eve, Andy and Maggie playing with Rambo. Andy had hold of the short leash on the dog's harness. It was difficult to tell who led whom. To Kylie, it seemed as if Rambo might be in charge.

Eve pushed forward in her chair several feet. "Andy, can you walk with Rambo toward the road."

From the corner of her eye, as she kept her attention on Andy, she saw Carson tense up. She didn't interfere. It was important that Rambo know his job and Andy know that his dog would protect him. It was also important that Carson trust the dog.

Trust was so important with a service dog.

Andy looked reluctant. His gaze shot to his dad and his lower lip might have trembled. Carson nodded.

Permission granted, Andy headed for the road some five hundred feet away. He wouldn't get there, of course, and they all knew it. Not only the dog, but the gate would keep him from leaving the property.

Kylie moved closer to Carson. He saw her and for a moment he seemed relieved, his features relaxed. Then he focused his attention back to Andy and Rambo. Kylie watched as Eve continued to move forward, with Maggie on her lap. The little girl held the sleeping puppy Skip in her lap.

As Andy wandered away from them, Rambo appeared to grow distressed. Without warning the dog sat, his whimper loud and clear even from a distance of one hundred feet. Andy tugged on the lead but Rambo wouldn't budge.

"Bring him back," Eve called out. "But pet him first."

Andy leaned to hug and pet his dog. He had no idea what the animal had done for him but the adults all knew.

"Thank you for this," Carson said softly, his voice gruff.

"For?"

He nodded toward Andy. "For Rambo. For changing my son's life."

"You're the one making decisions for him. And your dad—sorry, I mean Jack—suggested a dog."

"If you're reminding me of my manners, I do plan on thanking him before we go."

"Carson, you can't leave just yet. Andy needs time to learn how to work with Rambo. We're still working on new tasks for Rambo. He's a smart dog, but this is new territory for him." She paused, unsure of how to bring up the next subject. "And Jack. He needs you. He isn't going to tell you so, but he does."

"I'm not going to fall apart if you call him my father..."

"You call him Jack," she reminded. "I'm trying to respect that."

"I call him Jack because that's who he's been for most of my life. I haven't called anyone Dad or Father in twenty years."

She understood. She'd never met her father, and her mom's boyfriends, men who moved in and out of the trailer they'd called home, hadn't been father figures for her at all. She'd learned early on to study hard and to stay quiet and out of sight. She'd been the silent observer in her mother's life, determined to not turn into her mother.

The decision had been made the year she turned nine. She'd been upset with her mother and she'd said something about the way they lived. Her mom had laughed at her. "You think you're so high and mighty? Someday you'll be just like me."

"Earth to Kylie." It was Carson's voice, more recognizable because of the thread of laughter in his tone. "I remember that you used to always zone out like that."

Back then she'd been dreaming of him, of their adult life. And look at them now, standing side by side, not at all who she'd thought they'd be. Today they were just two people living different lives and going in different directions.

Chapter Nine

Carson hadn't forgotten the potluck Kylie mentioned that morning, but he'd tried. Unfortunately it appeared to be a ranch activity. They all loaded up in vehicles and headed to town. Carson drove his truck with Kylie sitting next to him. Jack had planned on going but changed his mind at the last second.

As they drove through town, Kylie asked him to make a brief stop at the lakeside resort and boat dock Jack planned to have up and running before the fishing tournament.

"Does Jack really think he's going to bring back the tourists?" Carson asked as they pulled into the resort parking lot. The dock was a short distance away.

"It isn't about bringing them back," Kylie informed him. "Grand Lake hasn't stopped drawing tourists. People come here to enjoy the lake, nature and other attractions. But Hope lost something. It got rundown, people stopped coming. It isn't so much about bringing back tourists as it is in rebuilding lives and families in the community. People need—" she grinned "—hope."

"That was cheesy," he said.

"Yeah, I know. But this place has been good for so many people. Look at the men and women at the ranch. The people in town are also inspired. The buildings on Shoreline Drive will be available to people who are looking to start out with no rent or overhead."

"It is a great plan."

"And you don't believe it will work. Maybe you should stay and be a part of it," she said. A small grin tipped her mouth and her eyes were warm, just a shade past honey in the dusky light of sunset.

Stay. No, he wouldn't go down that path. If he thought about staying, he thought about Kylie. And then he felt guilty. He felt unfaithful. He had a feeling Kylie had the same thought processes.

"I have to check and see if Matt brought the supplies they needed." Kylie opened the truck door. He saw a grimace as she moved to get out.

"Let me do this," Carson said as he moved to get out. "You stay with the kids."

She nodded and closed her door. "Thank you."

He got out and headed for the cabins that made up the Lakeside Retreat. A group of men were storing materials in a shed. One of them turned to wave as he approached.

"Hey, Doc." Lucas was the man's name. Carson had met him the previous day. "What brings you by here?"

"Kylie wanted to make sure the materials were delivered."

Lucas pointed inside the shed. "Matt brought them by today. I was going to tell Jack that someone has been messing around at the dock. The other day it was fishing poles. Today batteries from the new rental boats."

"Do we need to file a police report?" Carson asked.

"We think we know who did it." Lucas motioned him away from the other men. They walked down the hill toward the dock. "Donnie. He's been at the house but he's also been staying in town. I guess Kylie got him all riled up last week. I don't want to think he would hurt her, but just thought you ought to know."

Carson glanced back at his truck. The idea of someone hurting her. He didn't want to think about it.

"I'll keep an eye out," he told the other man. "If this continues, we need to report it."

"Yeah, I know. It's just..." Lucas shrugged. "We all look out for each other. We wouldn't want anything to happen to Kylie."

"I won't let anything happen to Kylie." He avoided meeting Lucas's eyes. "We're on our way to church. Let me know if you all need anything."

"Will do, Doc. Thanks."

With that, Carson headed back to his truck. He got in without saying anything and headed for the church on the outskirts of town. The church they'd sporadically visited as kids.

"Well?" Kylie asked after a few minutes.

"Matt delivered the stuff." He relaxed his grip on the steering wheel. "Donnie threatened you?"

She scrunched her face at that. "No, he was just angry. And that has nothing to do with the supplies Matt left."

"No, but it is important."

More important than he wanted to admit to himself. Admitting it would mean admitting she was still important to him.

"Donnie isn't going to hurt me. He's angry with life in general and that has nothing to do with anything I've done to him."

"If he shows up, if he threatens you, you need to file a report. And you can't hide this because we can't keep you safe if you don't tell us."

"Calm down."

He was calm. Calm as a man could be when he thought about letting someone down, not being there, making wrong choices. "I'm calm."

"Good thing. I'd hate to see you upset, though."

The tension fizzled. "Yeah, that wouldn't be too pretty."

He pulled into the church parking lot. Church. When he thought of church he thought about unanswered prayers. About the nightmare of losing Anna, of walking out of the hospital with a tiny baby girl. Alone.

"Are you okay?"

"I'm good."

"Hmm, yeah, I don't think so. What happened?"

"My wife died." He let the words, harsh and difficult, land between them. "And every prayer I prayed that night must have bounced off His deaf ears."

"Life is so hard." Her hand reached out and he let his fingers slide through hers. "God is real and pain is real. Heartache is real. Horrible, unfair things happen. But there is beauty from the ashes, Carson. Look in the seat behind you and tell me that little girl isn't beautiful."

He glanced in the rearview mirror, knowing he would see blond curls, brown eyes and the sweetest smile. He wanted to ask how Kylie had overcome her loss with such faith and dignity. But he realized that it hadn't been easy. She had her struggles. Most likely she had her own secrets, too.

"We should go in. I have the brownies. We won't be forgiven if I don't bring the brownies." She reached for the pan next to her. "I wouldn't have survived without faith. I still question. I still cry out at the unfairness of what I've lost. But I also know that life is beautiful."

She was beautiful, he thought. But it was better to focus on what was safe, what was real than on what could never be.

Kylie walked next to Carson. They neared the church and she saw the town mayor, Edna Parker, heading their way. She looked like a woman on a mission. But then again, just short of eighty years, and still going strong, Edna always appeared to be on a mission. She had recently told Kylie that at her age, she didn't have time to wait until tomorrow.

"Carson West, what a pleasure to see you here." Edna smiled big, her eyes sparkling. "Or should I call you *Dr.* West."

Carson released Maggie's hand for a moment to accept Edna's hand. "Carson is just fine."

Edna laughed. "I guess Jack hasn't convinced you to take on the clinic?"

"I'm not licensed in Oklahoma."

She shooed him away with her hand. "Stop it. You know you could get licensed with no trouble at all. You either want to. Or you don't. I don't know why people find that so difficult to understand."

"I'm a trauma surgeon, not a family practitioner."

This time Edna rolled her eyes. "I just want you to know, I'm praying for you. Whatever you decide, it is sure good to see you here in Hope."

"Thank you."

Edna hurried away. Carson cleared his throat. "No pressure."

Kylie laughed. "None at all. People are hopeful, you can't blame them for that. We have to drive all the way to Grove for the basics. It would be nice to have someone local."

"Then they should put an ad in the paper." Carson extended his elbow for her to take hold of as they climbed the steps. Andy moved ahead of them and out of the blue he reached for Maggie's hand. Carson hesitated just briefly. "That is a first."

"There are going to be more firsts," Kylie assured him. "I think having Rambo will open the world up for him."

They entered the fellowship hall where the end of the month potluck was being held. People were working in the kitchen. Others had already filled their plates.

"I have to take the brownies to the dessert table. You should get plates for Maggie and Andy." She stepped away from him.

There were people here that he remembered from his childhood. She knew that he would reconnect, find people to speak to and catch up with.

"We'll wait for you," he said, stopping her in her tracks, physically and emotionally.

She shook her head. "No, please go on."

If she allowed this, it would only hurt more when he left. Or if he stayed. Fortunately she didn't have to push him away. Isaac joined them, looking from one to the other, his eyes narrowed.

"Might as well get your food and sit with the rest of us," Isaac said. He actually held a hand out to Maggie. Kylie knew he wasn't much of a kid person. She thought he could be if he allowed himself.

"Who is *us*?" Carson asked.

"The crew from the ranch. A few locals. People you know that you've forgotten. Unless you're too good for us." Isaac left the insult hanging in the air.

"Why do you do that?" Carson asked.

Kylie knew why and she wanted to stop Isaac

from saying it. But he winked at her and she knew he couldn't be stopped.

He shrugged and pretended like it didn't matter. "I'm the replacement kid. But you're all he ever talked about."

Carson rubbed a hand across his jaw and studied Isaac for a long moment. "I'm sorry."

"Water under the bridge," Isaac said as he started to walk away. "Join us or not. Up to you."

"Go," Kylie urged. "I'll catch up with you in a bit."

He nodded, reached for Maggie and Andy, and followed the retreating back of his brother.

Kylie watched them go, then made a beeline for the safety of the kitchen. Today it didn't feel safe. She felt like she was surrounded by quicksand and no matter what, she was going under.

She'd been attending this church for several years and today was the first time she questioned her future here. From the beginning she'd felt at peace with the decision to help Jack with Mercy Ranch. She'd felt at peace in Hope.

Today she wondered what would happen if Carson and his children stayed in town. Not that Carson gave any indication that he would. But if he did?

Would she be able to keep her distance? Would she leave because that would be easier

than knowing he'd given his heart to someone else?

But if he left, would he take what remained of her heart?

Chapter Ten

Kylie woke up to the sound of a rooster crowing, and somewhere in the distance a horse whinnied. She eased out of bed, ashamed of how stiff she was. In the mornings, everything hurt. It didn't last, but for her it meant a slow start until the pain eased with stretching and movement.

She had earned the extra stiffness because she'd stayed at church the previous evening, volunteering to help clean up after the potluck. It had given her an excuse to find an alternate ride home.

The apartment was silent as she shuffled down the hallway to the kitchen and living area that the women shared. There were only four of them living there for the time being. Kylie, Eve, Miriam and Jules. Kylie had the only apartment on the ground floor. Because she'd lived there even before the idea of Mercy Ranch really took a firm hold. As the vision for the ranch grew, the housing grew with it. The garage had been given a second floor, elevator and four rooms upstairs with a small sitting room.

She put on a pot of coffee, but she wouldn't stay to have a cup. Instead she grabbed a bottle of water, one of Miriam's homemade power bars and a towel. It had been a few days since she'd worked out, and today her body was telling her she couldn't wait another day. As she headed for the door, she whistled for Rambo. But Rambo didn't come running.

She'd forgotten that Andy had been keeping Rambo at the main house. They'd wanted to give him time with Andy, just to make sure the two of them would work well together.

Her heart hurt a little from missing Rambo, but Skip joined her, stretching and then rolling on the floor as he left his small nighttime kennel. The puppy licked her feet and looked at her with plenty of adoration.

"Come on, Skip, time to exercise." She opened the door and stepped outside to a gray morning, clouds covering the sky.

Skip ran off to inspect a bush close up. She kept walking, leaning heavily on the cane she used in the mornings. She hated the thing but some days it was just necessary. Today happened to be one of those days.

The gym was empty. She used the keypad to unlock the door and entered with Skip running in behind her. She started to push him back outside but this morning she wanted the company. Between exercise and the puppy she could keep her mind off the pain, the past, the heartache.

She closed the door behind her, and for a moment she leaned against the wall and breathed deeply, eyes closed. She prayed, quietly in the silence, for mercy, for healing, for peace. She prayed for Jack and for his children and grandchildren. She prayed for the ranch and the community. As she prayed the anxiety ebbed; her heart felt a little lighter.

A knock on the door caused her to jump. Skip barked and ran around in a wild circle before forgetting about the danger and realizing he wanted to chase his tail.

"Who is it?" she asked, leaning close to the door.

"Carson."

She nearly groaned.

"Are you going to let me in?" he asked.

"Sure. Of course." She disarmed the alarm and let him in.

Pushing the door open, he stood on the other side looking refreshed, healthy, very male. He wore gym shorts, T-shirt and athletic shoes. He studied her as she studied him.

"You're not excited about company?" he asked.

"Not really," she said with honesty. "I mean, it's fine. I just usually get here before anyone else. Are Andy and Maggie sleeping?"

"No, they're with Jack. He's teaching them commands for Rambo. Probably not trainer-approved commands."

"Really?" she asked, hiding her amusement. "What commands are those?"

"He might be eating doughnuts."

She sighed. "I can't seem to convince him that dogs shouldn't eat sugar. You're up early."

"I'm always up early," he told her as he headed across the gym. He stopped midway and turned to wait for her. "What are you going to start with?"

"I'm not sure. Maybe the treadmill."

"Could I make a suggestion?"

"Sure, go ahead." She grabbed her towel, the cane and followed him across the room. He stopped at the open area where they typically did group exercise.

"Stretch your muscles. Also breathing is important."

"Breathing is definitely beneficial," she teased and pulled a smile from him. "I'm glad to see you can use those muscles this early in the morning."

"What muscles?"

She pointed to her mouth. "Facial muscles. You're the doctor—you must know that."

A big grin spread across his handsome face. "Yeah, I can smile. It isn't easy, working through all of this stuff with Jack and still trying to maintain some sort of structure for Andy and Maggie."

"I'm sure it isn't. But I think, no matter what you decide, you'll be glad you came here. There's something healing in forgiveness."

"Yeah," he said, but he didn't sound convinced.

"He has changed."

"I know he has." Carson studied her as he said it. "But haven't we all? Change happens whether we want it or not. Now, back to finding the best exercises for you. Breathing is beneficial to the muscles. As you stretch, you inhale and things loosen up. It can start out painful but I think you'll find that it gets a little easier with time."

"At this point, everything sounds painful," she admitted with as much humor as she could. After all, laughter was the best medicine.

Laughter was definitely better than the flush of heat she felt crawling up her neck as he surveyed her with a clinical look to his expression. At least there was no pity in his eyes. He no longer looked at her and saw the girl she'd been. That was for the best, she decided.

After all, it had been over twenty years ago, and what they'd known about real love could have fit into a thimble. It wasn't as if they'd been deeply in love and then torn apart. Instead, when he'd left, she had missed her best friend.

"If we do some easy stretches," he continued as if he hadn't noticed she'd been lost in the past, "I think you'll find it easier to move."

He took her cane and leaned it against the treadmill, then very gently he took her hand and helped her into what he must have considered an easy yoga pose. It included stretching her hands up and encouraging her to ease her knee up. He held her, making sure she didn't topple over if she lost her balance.

She closed her eyes because he told her to, and she took a deep breath. The action disguised the fact that she needed a moment to gather her wits, to distance herself from him emotionally, physically, the way it felt to have him so close to her. But at the moment, she had become a patient to him, nothing more. She reminded herself of that fact.

"Thank you," she whispered, thinking the

words would help solidify in her mind what she knew in her heart.

"You don't have to thank me. You're loaning us your dog. It means a lot to Andy. The mangy thing slept on his bed last night."

"He isn't mangy and you don't have to let him on the furniture."

He held her as she raised the opposite knee and took a deep breath. "Andy slept better than he has in years. Is it because of the dog's nearness?"

"I think so." She lowered her leg.

Carson still held her. His arms were around her, his hands on her back. The touch of a physician, she told herself. Then she called herself a liar. She'd been in and out of hospitals for four years. She'd had doctors, physical therapists, nurses and techs put their hands on her. Hands that helped her eat, helped her stand, then helped her walk. And not once had those hands, comforting as they might have been, undone something inside her, made her want a little more of him, his touch, his presence.

She told herself it would be enough, just to be held. If he decided to hold her, hug her. Then she'd back away and go about her day.

But when he did take that step forward, moving just a breath closer, close enough that his arms encircled her and his face lowered so that his lips met hers, she knew it wouldn't be enough. She knew she would want more of him than this kiss; she would want his heart. She would want his secrets. His pain. His laughter.

She would want the man she had known as a boy.

And that's where the dream ended because he wasn't that boy anymore, and his heart was no longer up for grabs. He'd given it to someone else. And then he'd lost her. Lost something beautiful. She didn't know if she'd ever truly had something beautiful. Her husband had been withdrawn for much of their marriage, sometimes happy, but mostly angry.

She pushed the thoughts away and regretted all the time she'd wasted overthinking things. The kiss. She focused on the kiss, on the arms that held her, on the strong shoulders her hands settled on. She didn't want this kiss to end. She wanted to still be the woman he dreamed of, wanted a future with. The kiss broke past the barriers she'd built around her heart, promised beauty and then just as quickly, reminded her of what she couldn't have. Suddenly she noticed tears trickling down her cheeks, salty as they brushed her lips.

His lips stilled, then moved to her cheek

where they brushed against her skin with a soft caress. She didn't want to be a mistake. Not again. She couldn't handle that again.

She didn't want another man to ever tell her they were a mistake. She wouldn't give Carson a chance to regret her.

She pulled back, already seeing regret in his eyes, dark and haunting.

"I'm sorry," he murmured as he put more distance between them. "I came to help you, not…" He shook his head. "Not this."

"It was nothing," she said lightly, wanting to let him off the hook.

"That isn't true," he said as he walked over to one of the treadmills. "It wasn't nothing."

She didn't argue. Because she couldn't really, could she. Not when the kiss had been everything. Their relationship would now be divided between two kisses. That remarkable first kiss at thirteen, when she thought they would always be together.

And then this beautiful kiss. *The kiss.* When she realized he would never be hers. He'd given his heart—his grown up heart—to someone else. And she couldn't resent that or be jealous, because Anna was gone. But she'd taken his heart with her.

And she still had hold of it. Even after all these years.

* * *

Carson needed a minute, maybe two to gather his thoughts. He hadn't meant to kiss Kylie. He'd meant to help her. The kiss had just happened. And boy, had it taken him by surprise.

If he was being truthful with himself, it had knocked him flat. He hadn't kissed anyone besides Anna almost eight years. And as he'd kissed Kylie, he couldn't help but think about the first and only time he'd kissed her, twenty years ago. They'd been running along the creek. He had pushed her in and when he'd offered to help her out of the water, she'd pulled him in with her. Laughing and holding hands, they'd climbed up out of the creek together. And he'd kissed her. It had been a sunny day in late spring. She'd held his cheeks with cold, wet hands as he did his best to kiss her.

Puppy love, that's what most adults would have called what the two of them had felt for each other. But it had been about the happiest summer of his life.

Guilt stabbed him. Because he had loved Anna. They had been happy together.

He felt guilty for kissing someone else. Guilty for enjoying the kiss.

The worst guilt of all, still simmering after three years, was knowing that if he hadn't been busy, if he'd gone to the store instead of her, she would still be alive today.

A hand touched his shoulder as he checked the controls on the treadmill. Pretended to check the controls. He knew how it worked and what he wanted it to do.

Her hand slid from his shoulder. He wanted to tell her. Everything. He had yelled at God. He had beaten himself up. He hadn't shared his most private thoughts. Ever. That he was the reason Anna had died. She'd been in the car accident because when she asked him to run to the store for milk, he'd told her he couldn't go. He'd been in the middle of researching a surgery.

And like a good surgeon's wife, she'd let him do the research, and did what needed to be done. She drove to the store herself. "Carson?" Kylie's voice was soft, tentative, just as her hand on his shoulder had been. "Don't beat yourself up."

"Oh, believe me, I can and I do." He reached for her hand and brought her closer to the machine. "Slow and no incline. I don't want you to fall."

"I won't fall. You know, I do this almost every day."

"I'm sure you do."

She gave him a teasing look. "But today the doctor is in charge."

"Yes," he said.

Without argument she stepped on the treadmill and allowed him to adjust everything. As she walked, he made for the kickboxing equipment in the corner. Not usually his exercise of choice but today it fit his mood.

He punched the freestanding bag a few times, then backed up for a moment to catch his breath. From the corner of his field of vision he saw movement. A moment later Kylie stood to the side of the leather bag. She leaned on her cane and watched as he kicked, then jabbed the bag.

After a few minutes he stopped, waiting for her to say whatever was clearly on her mind.

"I'm going to Jack's house to fix breakfast."

"Jack already did. Pancakes and sausage."

"Oh, okay. Well, I guess I'm going to eat *his* breakfast, then. I have a few counseling sessions today and I told Jack I would run to town later for supplies." She was still giving him that very pointed look.

"Is that all?" he asked.

She shook her head. "No, but I'm trying to be cautious how I say this."

"Just say it. If it's about kissing you, I won't let that happen again."

"That wasn't it, but thanks for letting me know."

Now she looked hurt. "Kylie, I'm sorry."

She held up a hand to stop him. "Promise

that if you ever need to talk, you will. Either with me, or someone else. I don't care who. Just don't..." Her eyes reflected the past, the pain. "Don't let it eat away at you. I know you loved Anna and you miss her. I just don't want you to..."

He got it. He considered himself an intelligent person. He even thought of himself as observant. But he had missed the obvious. He had missed that Kylie would be sensitive to other people, to their sadness, to anything she thought might be depression. Because of her husband, Eric. The two of them shared more than a past. They shared similar stories, similar heartache.

"I'm going to leave you alone to fight this battle. But if you ever need to talk, I'm here."

He let her walk away but when she reached the door he stopped her, because he couldn't let her worry about him, about his mental state.

"Kylie."

She glanced back, her hand on the door. "Yes?"

"I'm fine. You don't have to worry about me. Yes, I miss Anna. Yes, I worry about my children. And sometimes I do feel guilty. But I'm okay."

"I know you are." She swiped at her cheek and her gaze dropped to the floor. "I know that you're fine. But I worry all of the time. It's what

I do. What if someone isn't fine and I overlook the symptoms? Or if they tell me they're okay and they're not?"

"You have to realize that you can't fix everyone. And you can't control other people's actions. You do your best with the information you're given."

"I know you're right." She looked up, focusing on the ceiling and blinking back tears. Finally she took a deep breath and looked at him. "I know you're right. I tell myself every day that I use the skills I have, and I trust God with the rest."

Trusting God. That was the part where he struggled. Knowledge flickered in her eyes and she sighed.

"You blame God for what happened, don't you?"

"God and myself. I'm working on forgiveness because Andy and Maggie need for me to be the best person I can be. If I'm going to drag them somewhere to start a new life, it has to be a *new* life."

"You're a good dad. I hope you know that."

"Thank you." He kissed the top of her head. "I'll walk with you to the house."

She nodded, then bent down to pick up Skip, who had fallen asleep on a mat next to the door.

They walked out the door to absolute chaos.

He didn't know how they hadn't heard the shouting that was coming from the arena. As they headed that way, it appeared an all-out brawl might be taking place.

"It's Donnie."

"What?" he asked as they picked up speed.

"Donnie. We've been working through some anger but I'm starting to think he needs more help than we can give him. We want to help them all, but the ranch isn't equipped for more serious situations."

The big guy with the angry scowl and large hands that were wrapped around Isaac's throat had to be Donnie. Before Carson could stop her, Kylie was through the gate and heading straight for the fight. One man was already on the ground. Isaac appeared to be losing and Kylie was going in strong.

Carson jumped the fence and moved between her and obvious danger. She pushed at him.

"Get out of my way."

"You can't poke a bear and not suffer the consequences."

"Just watch me."

With that, she plowed forward and poked Donnie in the gut with her cane.

"Stop."

He wouldn't have guessed such a loud voice could come from such a small woman. If the situation hadn't been so serious, he might have laughed. As it was, he could only act. And that meant hurrying forward as Isaac fell to the ground.

"What in the world is going on here?" She poked Donnie again. He growled and took a step toward her.

"I wouldn't if I were you, man." Carson stood there, knowing he might be as tall as the other man but if it came to a fight, he would lose. He didn't have the body mass or the anger on his side.

"People need to stay out of my business." Donnie wiped at the spittle on the corner of his mouth.

"Yeah, I understand that." Carson glanced at his brother and a younger man, one he hadn't met. They were conscious and recovering their senses. He focused on the unfriendly giant standing in front of him.

"I'm going to kill you, Isaac West. You don't get in a man's business."

"But if the business is dealing drugs on this ranch, Donnie, you're the one in the wrong," Kylie said.

In the distance Carson heard the sound of sirens. Donnie lunged for Kylie but Carson blocked him, taking a blow to his jaw from the solid steel fist.

He didn't go down but he couldn't have been happier to see the police pull up. He grabbed Kylie and tried to keep her from becoming the next victim. She didn't cling to him, and he wouldn't have expected her to. But she did lean into him for just a moment.

That made him realize that life had a way of taking a man by surprise. And so did people.

Chapter Eleven

Jack didn't appear with Maggie and Andy until after the patrol car left with Donnie. Carson still felt shaken inside, thinking of those hands on Kylie's neck. He shouldn't have allowed her anywhere near the arena. Not that he could have stopped her. But he could have tried.

"Do we need an ambulance?" Jack asked as he eased through the gate, first telling Andy and Maggie to stay put with Rambo. He pointed at the dog. "Stay."

Rambo sat and the children plopped down next to him.

"I think I'm good," Isaac rasped, rubbing at his throat. "Man, he's strong. Check Jason, he took the worst of it."

Carson glanced at Kylie. She nodded in answer to his question. "I'm fine, Carson."

He squatted in front of Jason. The guy was

younger, midtwenties, with a buzz cut, lean cheeks and a good-sized bruise on his forehead.

"Did he hit you with his fist or something else?" Carson asked as he examined the guy. "Can you follow my finger with just your eyes?"

He held his finger in front of Jason and moved it back and forth. Jason followed but his hand went to his head and he flinched. "I'm good. It's Thursday. You're Carson. My head hurts because he doesn't need any other weapon. He has a fist that feels like a brick."

Carson chuckled. "Yeah, I met that fist. Let's get you an ice pack and something for the headache you have, or will have very soon."

"What happened to set him off?" Jack asked as he leaned in to give Isaac a good look. "Were you teasing him again?"

"He was trying to sell Aaron a bottle of pills."

Kylie sighed. "He didn't buy them, did he?"

"No," Jason answered. "He's good. Don't worry. If you all don't mind, I'm going to my room."

Carson offered the younger man his hand and pulled him to his feet. "Any blurring vision or dizziness, come find me."

He turned his attention to Isaac. "You. Take a deep breath."

"Take a hike," Isaac shot back with a grin.

"Glad to know you're okay. How's your throat?"

Isaac shrugged and got to his feet. “Fine. A little hoarse but there’s not much you can do for that.”

“No, not much.”

Another broad grin. Isaac poked at Carson’s cheek, making him flinch. “Might want to do something about your face. You’ve got a gash on your cheek and a big bruise on your jaw.”

Carson started to comment about his face but he didn’t have time; instead he reacted, reaching for Isaac as the other man staggered and stumbled.

“Are you okay?”

Isaac didn’t answer him. All he did was jerk his arm free from the hold Carson had on him.

“I asked if you’re okay.”

“Isaac, answer the man or the next call I make is for an ambulance,” Kylie chimed in, worry in her voice.

That got Isaac’s attention. He pulled off his cowboy hat and ran a hand over his military short hair. He took a deep breath and touched his ear. The ear that connected to the jagged scar on the side of his head.

“What did you say?” Isaac asked, his gray eyes troubled as he met Carson’s gaze.

“I asked if you’re okay. Obviously you aren’t.”

“I’m fine. Just an old injury. It knocks me a little off-balance from time to time.”

"Maybe something we need to check out?" Carson asked.

"Nope, I'm fine." Isaac gave him a grin to prove the point. Carson wasn't convinced but he knew that pushing wouldn't get him anywhere.

"I'm going to walk this off," Isaac said to Jack. "Don't worry, I'm fine."

"Yeah, yeah. Everyone here is fine." Jack's worried gaze fell on Carson and then Kylie. "The two of you might want to head to the house. Kylie, you look frazzled and Carson might need stitches."

Carson touched the tender spot on his cheek. He came away with blood on his fingers. "What was that guy on?"

Kylie shook her head. "My guess? Meth. We've caught him with prescription pills and I thought maybe we could help him, but a lot of his problems are due to his teen years and not injuries suffered in battle. People have pasts. Often those pasts get jumbled together with trauma suffered in the military."

Carson understood that. People were a lot like their physical symptoms. A person could come to him with a basketful of symptoms and think they were suffering from one illness. Many times that wasn't the case. Some people suffered layer after layer of injury and illness, and it took some unraveling to figure out which illness caused each symptom.

"I need to take care of the kids," Carson told Kylie when she tried to lead him away.

"Jack could take them to the swings while I get you cleaned up," she suggested.

Jack nodded his agreement. "I don't mind at all. And after you're cleaned up, we'll make a trip to town. And Kylie, you know that Donnie can't come back. Next time he might hurt you or one of the other women. We can't have him here on the ranch anymore."

"I know." She looked heartbroken.

Carson watched as Jack returned to where Maggie and Andy waited with Rambo. The dog had stood as Jack approached and he nudged Andy a little, getting the child's attention. It had been only a couple of days but already he could see the positive impact the dog was having on Andy's life.

Jack held a hand out to Maggie and said something to Andy that had Carson's son glancing back at him. He waved and nodded, giving Andy the reassurance he needed. It worked. Andy grinned and hurried alongside Jack.

Carson wanted to see those smiles every single day. He just hoped that they wouldn't disappear when they left Oklahoma. He hoped that staying on the ranch so Andy could work with

Rambo wouldn't ultimately make things more difficult for his children. He wanted them to leave here with good memories and not with bruised hearts.

"They're fine, you know," Kylie assured him. She'd misunderstood his concerned looks.

"I know they are." He could be honest with her. He knew that. "I just worry about what'll happen when we leave. Staying isn't part of my plan. I thought I'd come up here and see what Jack had to say and then we'd be on our way. I hadn't expected you to be here."

She pulled back a bit and shook her head. "What do I have to do with any of this?"

She no longer leaned on the cane. He assumed because she'd been moving a while and the stiffness had finally abated.

"You're pretty effective using that thing as a weapon. I'm almost afraid of you."

She flashed a grin at him. "I won't hurt you. Too much."

He wasn't so sure about that.

"Go on," she encouraged, nudging his arm with hers. "You hadn't expected me to be here. What does that have to do with anything?"

"You're easy to get attached to," he finally said, clearing his throat. "Andy and Maggie are getting attached to you. That will make it more difficult for them when we have to leave."

"I know you're trying to protect them, Carson. That's admirable. But you can't protect them from everything. What you can do is prepare them. Prepare them for disappointments, for heartache, for change. It's simple. They need to know that I'm here to help them with Rambo, but when you move to Chicago, I won't be there. Jack won't be there. The ranch won't be there. But there will be other things that will be there. And most important you'll be there."

"You're right," he agreed. "But you don't get what it's like. When something awful happens and you don't have time to prepare a child. Andy was two when Anna was killed. He didn't understand. I think he still doesn't understand."

"He's a smart boy, and close to five now, isn't he?"

Carson nodded.

"He probably has questions. You can talk to him, help him to understand better, more at his age level, now that he is older."

He agreed; he could do that. He needed to do that. He would have asked Kylie to help but that would have dragged her deeper into their lives.

And he had a feeling that that wasn't really where she wanted to be.

As they walked toward Jack's house Kylie wondered if she had gone too far, giving advice where it wasn't wanted or needed. She also considered what he said about the children getting too attached to her, making it difficult for them when they had to leave. She understood that. A selfish part of her wished Carson hadn't stayed. She wished Jack hadn't suggested a service dog for Andy.

They were sweet, beautiful kids. And Carson was kind and decent. But they were complications she didn't need in her life right now.

"Are you second-guessing your advice?" Carson asked as they walked up the sidewalk to the house.

She looked at him and felt a little reassured because he didn't look angry. He didn't sound angry.

"A little, yes."

"Don't. You're right. I know I need to talk to Andy. I know I need to help them adjust. Maybe while we're here..."

He didn't finish, but she knew the way he would have finished that sentence if Eve hadn't headed their direction from their apartment. He had been about to ask her to take part in the discussion he would have with his children. He'd been about to draw her further into their lives. It was a place she wanted to be, but couldn't. She didn't belong there.

An hour ago he had kissed her and she'd seen

the guilt etched in his expression. She knew how that felt and she didn't want that emotion tagged to a possible relationship between them.

"I heard about the fight," Eve said as she wheeled up to them. "Looks like you stepped in front of a truck."

Carson grinned, but then he flinched and he touched his cheek. "Yeah, kind of feels that way."

"We're heading back to get it bandaged up right now," Kylie offered.

"Good idea, because that is really disgusting to look at." She grinned. "It's like someone took a beautiful work of art and threw paint on it."

"Oh, please," Kylie muttered.

Eve laughed. "It had to be said."

"No. Really, it didn't."

"Kind of did." Eve winked at Carson. "But I'm not an art thief."

"We have to go now," Kylie stated, glaring at her friend.

"Oh, wait, I didn't just come over here to tease you. I came to let the two of you know they're having the pie auction at the church. You weren't there the Sunday they finalized the details."

"When is it?" Kylie didn't remember anything about a pie auction, but then, she'd been distracted lately.

"Tonight, silly. The Bluegrass Bills are going to be playing music and ladies from the community have donated pies. It's a fun time. The money goes to Hope Group Home."

She had forgotten. The group home for teens had been in operation for nearly a year, and few people knew that Jack had given them the initial start-up money and continued to be the major donor. She shouldn't have forgotten the pie auction. Maybe she had because the idea of it kind of gave her the willies. The pie auction was a couple's thing.

"Are we going?" Carson asked.

Eve grinned. "Oh, definitely. Everyone will be there. And I baked two apple pies for the occasion. One for myself and one for Kylie."

"I'm not taking a pie," Kylie told her friend. "I'll donate money."

"You have to take a pie," Eve continued. No one could ever say that Eve wasn't determined.

Kylie narrowed her eyes at her friend. "I'll talk to you in a little while. Let me get this taken care of."

"Now you're a 'this,'" Eve teased, then spun around and headed back to the apartment.

"From 'work of art' to a 'this.' I'm not sure how to feel about the very quick demotion in rank." Carson put a hand to her back and guided her up the stairs. She had a very real urge to stomp on his toe. Just once. Maybe she could use the cane that she had under her arm.

Instead she exhaled and led Carson to the laundry room, which was also their makeshift infirmary with first aid supplies, cold medicines and other items.

"Have a seat." She pointed to a stool near the sink.

Carson glanced in the mirror over the sink and cringed. "I never saw his fist coming."

"He also doesn't have a shutoff valve." She grabbed gauze, paper towels, antiseptic and other supplies from the cabinet.

"None of that is going to work." He pulled at the wound to examine it, flinching a little at his own touch.

Kylie ripped open a disposable wipe that would clean and disinfect. "Here, let me."

He sat down on the stool and she wished he would close his eyes. Instead he watched, his gray eyes studying her face as she wiped the wound. She touched his cheek to hold him steady but the minute her fingers made contact with his skin, she knew it was a mistake.

"It's deep." She didn't need to tell him that but she had needed to say something to break the silence between them.

"Do you have a butterfly bandage in that bag of tricks?"

She dug around in the bag and realized it was sadly in need of restocking. He laughed a little and she looked up, questioning with her eyes.

"You're so focused on your search, you're biting your lip and scrunching your nose. For a second I thought you were thirteen again and hunting for arrowheads by the creek."

"That was a long time ago."

"Yes, it was." He agreed in a voice that took a faraway tone.

The days he'd spoken of didn't seem real. She'd been a different person with different dreams. If she could make him understand how happy this ranch made her, how content she was living here. She wanted to keep that happiness intact.

He reached in the bag and pulled out what she'd been looking for and hadn't seen. "Let's just use this one."

"You distracted me," she accused.

"Did I?"

"Stop," she told him. A pleading tone had entered her voice. She refused to be that person. "I can't do this."

"Do what?" He stood to look at himself in the mirror as he put the skin back together with the butterfly bandage.

"Flirt. I can't pretend my past away. I can't pretend good health or..." She had to stop there before she said too much. She didn't want sympathy. She didn't want pity. She wanted understanding. She wanted…so many things.

"I know." His voice softened as he said it and he reached to curl a strand of her hair around his fingers.

"We're here today because we've both been through things, difficult things. You're trying to start over somewhere. And I'm happy with my life. I love it here." Honesty. She had to give him that. He deserved the truth. "For the first time in my life, I am truly happy. I don't want anything to jeopardize that."

"I'm not here to jeopardize your happiness."

She glanced at their reflection in the mirror and saw that it was too intimate, the two of them in that small room together. She carried the bag to the cabinet and made herself stand there for a minute rearranging, organizing.

"Kylie?"

"You have no idea how your presence here could jeopardize things for me. I don't want to look at you, at your children, and see what I can't ever have. I'd rather keep focusing on what I do have," she said, facing him. "I just want to be thankful for everything I have and enjoy what I've been given."

She stopped. She couldn't tell him the rest, no matter how much she believed in being honest and upfront. He didn't need to hear that she was already attached to his children. And they would be gone soon, the three of them. She knew she could survive it, she could survive just about anything, but she didn't want to always be surviving.

She wanted children. She wanted babies. And she couldn't have them. Seeing Carson with Maggie and Andy, she envied him. And she didn't want to envy him. He did have beautiful children, but life hadn't been easy for him or for Maggie and Andy. "I have to go. I have things to do." She started walking away from him.

"Kylie," he called out, but she didn't stop. She couldn't stop. She wasn't going to cry in front of him. She wasn't going to cry, period.

Chapter Twelve

"Where's Kylie?" Carson asked as he came downstairs a short time later.

Jack had returned to the house with the kids. Maggie and Andy were playing with toy horses and a miniature farm truck and livestock trailer. They were loading and unloading the tiny horses on the trailer.

Jack jerked a bit as he sat in the chair, his hand trembling as he held it against his stomach.

"You've been overdoing it, Jack. Because you feel as if you have to do everything." Carson sat in the chair next to the recliner. "We don't have to go to town, you know."

"I'm going to town. I have to try Holly's new dessert at the restaurant. She's downright proud of this vanilla bread pudding recipe she created."

"I bet she is. It isn't every day that someone

discovers another way to block more arteries and increase your heart disease."

Jack guffawed at that and even slapped his knee. "Make me a cup of coffee. I'm going to tell Holly to call that dessert the Jack Attack."

"Great." Carson walked away. "Decaf."

"No decaf. And after that dessert at the café, I'm going to the pie auction. I'm bidding on Lana Gold's pumpkin streusel pie. She's a pretty gal, that Lana is."

"You're seventy years old and you're having open heart surgery in a few weeks."

"So she'll inherit things sooner rather than later."

He pushed the button on the coffeemaker and the cup filled with dark brew that smelled pretty good. "I don't see anything to joke about."

"No, of course not. Sorry," Jack mumbled as he took the cup of coffee Carson offered. "I'm sorry I wasn't there."

Carson glanced past his father and saw that Maggie and Andy had headed to the family room with their toys.

"We lived a whole life without you. That's the part I don't understand. You gave Mom custody. I get it. That was the deal. She stayed and she got her payment. And she got us. But it would have been nice to see you once in a while. When you got sober, why couldn't you have looked us up?"

"I signed a paper saying I would stay away. If I hadn't, she could have taken everything."

"So you chose to step aside."

"You had a decent life with her and...what's his name."

"His name was Parker. Allan Parker." Carson ground the name out. "And we had a decent life, but there were things..." Carson shook his head. "I'm not going to get into all that with you. Not right now."

Andy wandered into the kitchen, the toy truck and trailer in his small hands. He held them out to Carson. "Daddy, fix them?"

"You bet I will." He hooked the trailer and truck, then unhooked it, showing Andy how it worked. "Did you have fun on the swings?"

Andy nodded, his gaze on the truck and trailer. "I want to ride real horses."

Carson smoothed his son's hair. "We can do that."

"I like the ranch." Andy bit down on his bottom lip and his gaze shifted to Jack.

Carson knew that look. Andy liked the ranch. He loved his grandpa Jack. How could Carson ever explain to his children that this place couldn't be their home?

From the beginning he'd had a plan that included a job, a home and schools that would make their lives better. A place free of memories. Hope didn't qualify on any level.

Jack raised his coffee cup and it shook badly, spilling a little liquid down the front of his shirt. "I need a sippy cup."

It proved to be a much needed distraction, taking his mind off the way Andy looked hopeful, and the way Carson felt like no matter what, he would let his children down by making the wrong choices for their future.

"There are things we can do to help you with the Parkinson's. There are medications you can take."

"I don't want them. Side effects."

"You have to weigh the disease against the side effects." Stubborn. That much hadn't changed.

"Right, I'll just get a sippy cup."

Carson reached to help him lift the coffee cup to his lips. "There are cups made for Parkinson's patients. I'll order you one."

Jack nodded and set the cup on the table next to his chair. "I never thought this would be my life. I've always been strong and healthy."

"I know." Or at least he assumed he was.

"I want your forgiveness, Carson. I know I don't deserve it. I guess mercy isn't earned or deserved. But God knows we need it."

Carson could agree with that. He knew the dark paths his own anger had taken him down. He knew that Jack had traveled his own paths and some had been pretty difficult to navigate.

Vietnam. Carson couldn't imagine the nightmare of being a kid from Oklahoma suddenly dropped in a jungle with enemies on all sides.

"Carson, I was there."

"What? Where were you?"

"For each graduation. For your wedding. For Daisy's appendectomy. When Colt got in trouble with the law. For Anna's funeral. I was there."

"This is probably the wrong way and the wrong time to tell me," Carson said. He looked at Andy and Maggie, and thought about the moments to come for his children. He planned on being at each and every one of them. He couldn't imagine anything stopping him.

But being there and not telling them? Did that make it better somehow, that Jack was there, somewhere in the background, perhaps watching from a car in the distance?

"We should go to town. Holly's waiting to serve you up a heaping slice of the Jack Attack." Carson dropped his gaze to focus on his children. "Maggie and Andy, let's put the toys in the box now."

Andy shook his head and kept playing.

"Andy, we have to go."

Again he shook his head. Maggie got up and reached for a horse. Andy grabbed it and held it away from her. Maggie leaned close. "Andy, please."

Andy slumped and nodded his head. Maggie took the toys and put them in the box and then she grabbed Andy's hand. Would it always be this way, with the younger sister leading the older brother? Carson prayed for Andy to have the best life possible, the life God wanted for him. And he prayed for Maggie, that she would always love and be understanding of her brother.

He didn't know what else to do, other than to pray. He couldn't fix things for his children. He could only make the best decisions possible for them. And the rest had to be up to God, His plan and His timing.

Rambo stood and moved to Andy's side. Without hesitation the child took the handle of the harness and he petted Rambo's head.

"Rambo, good boy, Rambo." Andy whispered the words close to the dog's ears. Rambo perked up and moved a little closer to his tiny human.

"Best decision ever," Jack said. "That's something we can agree on."

Maggie took his hand and the four of them plus Rambo walked out the side door to the garage. Carson stood at the bottom of the steps and watched as his dad held the rail and slowly, gingerly, eased himself down.

Maggie stopped on the bottom step of the garage. “Kylie?”

“She’s staying here. We’ll see her later.” Jack rested, leaning against the front of the truck. Maggie held her arms up to him. “Lift that little girl up so I can give her a hug. Those hugs are worth more than gold.”

Carson agreed and he lifted Maggie to hug her grandfather. Then his mind switched to thoughts of Kylie. “I’m going to back the car out and then I’m going to check on Kylie.”

“Leave her be, Carson. She needs a little space,” Jack informed him as he got in the passenger side of the Escalade. “You make her think about things.”

“Things?”

Jack coughed a little. “Yeah, well, you know… the past, stuff.”

“Worst answer ever.” Carson started the SUV and backed out of the garage. “Are you saying I shouldn’t go looking for her?”

Jack shrugged. “I missed out on a lot of years of giving you advice, so yeah, I guess that’s what I’m saying. Sometimes you have to give a woman space.”

“Thanks for the advice.” He grinned as he shifted the SUV into Drive.

As he headed down the driveway, he saw her. She was in the garden kneeling over plants, a small watering can in her hand and a basket next to her. He thought of Eve's statement about works of art and he thought perhaps he'd never seen anything as sweetly beautiful as Kylie in the garden with pink gloves on her hands and her hair held back with a pink bandanna.

He glanced in the rearview mirror and saw that Andy had spotted her, too. His son smiled sweetly, a smile that said he'd seen someone important to his life. Carson ignored the flutter of emotion in his own heart at the thought. Every day they stayed here at Mercy Ranch increased the chance that one of them or all of them would be hurt.

He wasn't quite sure what to do about that.

Kylie and Eve had planned to go right to the church for the pie auction. But somehow they'd miscalculated the time and arrived in town an hour early. That left them nowhere to go but Mattie's Café. That was the last place she wanted to be. As Kylie and Eve sat in her car staring at the building that had been a general store in the early 1900s, she saw Andy, Maggie, Jack and Carson through the window. Holly stood at their table, her wide smile in place as she shared one of her stories. Holly loved telling stories.

And everyone loved Holly. Including Kylie. She had nothing against the woman. She told herself she wasn't jealous of the way Carson threw his head back and laughed at the end of the tale.

And she wasn't jealous of the way Holly's hand went to his shoulder.

"Are we going in?" Eve asked.

She'd forgotten Eve. "Sure, why not?"

"Because you don't want to get involved. But you are involved, honey. *Very* involved. In fact, I think you've kissed him." Eve laughed when Kylie shot her a withering look. "Maybe more than once. And now you're questioning the wisdom of that and worrying about how it will feel when he leaves."

"Shut up."

"Did you ever stop to think, what if he doesn't leave?"

"He'll leave. And it doesn't matter. Stay or go, there can't be anything between us. He has his children. I have the ranch. We have nothing in common."

"You have everything in common. You have a past in common. You have a love for Jack and for Carson's children. You have chemistry in common. Feelings in common."

"Stop." Kylie put fingers to her temples. "Shhh. You're giving me a headache."

"Since when does honesty give you a headache?"

"I can't have children. My body tells me every day that it won't ever recover from what that bomb did to it."

Eve rolled her eyes and pointed to the wheelchair in the back seat of the car. "Reminder, I can't walk."

"I'm sorry, that was selfish of me. I shouldn't have had the pity party."

"No, you shouldn't have. But if anyone can understand, I can. Do you know how much I miss riding horses? I miss jogging. I miss yoga."

"I know." Kylie put a hand on Eve's arm. "I know."

"But I can have babies. I know that's the heart of this, Kylie. I know how much you want that."

She nodded, closing her eyes and pinching the bridge of her nose. "I really do. And I try not to be jealous or mean when people have babies. Or when I see children. It's just… I want them so badly."

"I know that this is going to sound, I don't know, clichéd? But God loves you more than I ever could and He knows the desires of your heart, honey."

"But He can't make my uterus reappear." She

laughed a little. Because it was better to laugh than to cry.

"No, but He can give you children. Maybe not children you carry in your body, but children that you will love and they'll fill every empty space in your heart." Eve reached for her hand. "I'm sorry, I don't mean to minimalize your pain. I just want you to be happy. I'm used to you being the one cheering me up and I'm not very good at this role."

"You're actually really good at this. Thank you."

"I have a very wise friend and she's rubbed off on me. I used to be selfish and strong-willed. Okay, I'm still both of those things from time to time. But I'm much nicer than I used to be."

"You are very nice," Kylie quipped.

"So let's go inside the café and see what the Picasso is up to."

"The Picasso?" Kylie rolled her eyes at Eve's reference to Carson. "You realize he did portraits with misshaped faces, eyes on the sides of their heads and two noses?"

"Yeah, yeah. We'll just call him the walking work of art, then. I know he's yours," she said, holding a hand up when Kylie tried to object. "He's yours, but I can still look and think that God has created something beautiful."

"Oh boy," Kylie said as she got out to pull

the wheelchair from the back of the car for Eve. She opened the passenger door and continued the conversation. "And he *isn't* mine. I am *not* looking for a relationship. Me and God, we're in this together and I'm very content."

Eve laughed as she transferred herself to the chair. She grabbed her purse off the passenger seat and closed the car door.

"You're an honest person, Kylie. Be honest with yourself."

"I am. I know exactly what I have and what I want. Carson West was a part of my childhood, my past, not my present. Having him here does nothing to change the fact that I'm very happy with the life I have right now."

"And what about your future?"

"I'll still be at Mercy Ranch. And Carson will be in Chicago working as a surgeon."

"Okeydokey, if that's the way you're writing the story, we'll go with your not-so-happy ending."

Kylie pushed the chair up the ramp and through the door of the café. Holly waved a greeting as she headed through the double doors of the kitchen. Suddenly Rena, the waitress who had been at the café "since forever," hurried out holding a tray with two waters perched on top of it.

"Hey, girls, find a table and I've got your water," Rena called out as she grabbed menus.

"Kylie," Andy yelled as she and Eve headed for an empty table.

She waved at the little boy. Carson pushed back his chair and stood. "Are the two of you going to join us?"

Eve gave her a knowing look, then she moved forward. "Of course we are. Make room, Jack, I'm sliding in next to you."

"You keep that up and I might just bid on your pie, Eve." Jack winked as he said it. "But then, that might keep some young fella from bidding on it. We wouldn't want that, would we?"

"I don't think anyone will be bidding on my pie, Jack. They're all too afraid of me."

Rena set the water down in front of Eve and Kylie. "Are you two eating? We have grilled chicken salad. I think she adds some fruit and stuff that no self-respecting country girl would want."

"I have no self-respect," Eve said. "I'd like a bacon cheeseburger and fries. Hold the ketchup."

"That's my girl. Eat the good stuff. Kylie?" Rena tapped her pen on the order pad. "I guess you want that salad with the rosemary something-or-other dressing?"

"Organic. Don't forget that part." Kylie held

the menu out to the waitress. "I'm a creature of habit."

"Yes, you are, dear. I hope you'll at least try the Jack Attack." Nearing sixty, with short gray hair and bright blue eyes, Rena smiled at Jack as she mentioned the dessert.

Eve laughed, and the sound was so contagious, people at other tables joined in. "Jack Attack?"

"Vanilla bean bread pudding. With raspberries and white chocolate on top. I think it's got about a thousand calories a slice."

"Count me in," Eve told the waitress. "But make it to go, please. I wouldn't want to overdo it."

Kylie had taken the seat next to Andy. The little boy slid his drawing in front of her and she leaned to tell him it was very good. He grinned and, without speaking, drew a tic-tac-toe game in the empty space on the paper. Kylie picked up a red crayon and drew an *X*. He marked a square with a green *O*. Across the table she met Carson's gaze. He winked at her. Her stomach did a funny flip.

Their food arrived and Kylie helped Andy with his burger while Carson helped Maggie. She didn't want to think about how natural it felt, but of course the thought ran through her mind. If things had been different, she might have had children of her own by now.

Those weren't the thoughts she wanted. Not today.

She looked up and realized she had an audience. Carson was watching her. The corner of his mouth lifted but the gesture didn't quite reach his eyes. Those eyes were troubled, or perhaps *regretful* might have been a better word.

They were two sides of the same coin, Carson and her. They were both fighting off memories of the past, both looking for the right path to the future, but each finding different ways to deal with what they'd been through.

Carson seemed to be searching for a way back to faith and trying hard to make the right choices for the future of his family.

She already had faith. She needed God the way she needed air. She might sometimes get blue or angry, but He was always just a prayer away. He gave her peace when things seemed to be falling apart around her.

She glanced away from Carson and smiled down at Andy who had drawn another picture. This time of what was obviously his dog. He even leaned over to show the picture to Rambo, who was sitting obediently next to his chair.

Peace. She breathed in, breathed out, reminding herself that this was only temporary. Soon, everything would get back to normal. Carson and the children would leave, and she would find a way to continue on as she had before they arrived.

But before she hadn't known how much their presence would add to her life. It might be harder to move on than she'd thought.

Chapter Thirteen

The church parking lot overflowed with cars, trucks and even a few bikes. Carson got out of his SUV and unbuckled Maggie from her car seat. On the opposite side, Jack managed to get Andy out of his seat.

But he did it with no small amount of grumbling.

"Stupid seats," he said at one point. Then he winked at Andy. "Back when I was a kid…"

Carson cut him off. "Don't say it, Jack. Soon you'll be having them thinking they can stand up or ride on the roof."

Andy laughed and when he laughed, Maggie laughed. Her blond hair was getting a little long and framed her face in wild disarray. He needed to get her to Wilma, the only beautician in town. Although Eve had tried to convince him that she was decent with scissors. He wasn't sure how much he trusted Eve since she had also offered to give him a haircut and assured him she was a pro with hair clippers.

"I wasn't gonna say any such thing," Jack said as he offered Andy a hand getting down from the SUV. "I just think there should be an easier way to get kids in and out of those contraptions."

"Easier might not be safer," Carson countered.

"Oh, brother, you just want to argue with me." Jack stood back as Andy grabbed his dog. "Andy, does he ever argue with you?"

Andy, solemn but with a hint of a smile, shook his head.

"Now, I find that hard to believe."

Carson and Maggie joined Andy and Jack and they all proceeded toward the church. As they neared the door of the big fellowship hall, Carson spotted Kylie and Eve with Isaac. The three of them were talking, laughing, and totally at ease with one another.

He realized he was the odd man out. He didn't know how to be single. Isaac was an expert at teasing and flirting. He stood there in his faded jeans, brown cowboy boots and white cowboy hat tipped low over his face and he worked the crowd the way a politician would his constituents.

Jack stumbled a bit on a rough patch of ground and Carson reached out to steady him.

"Thank you," Jack grumbled. "It's no fun getting older."

"You could use that cane Isaac made you. It'll give you a little help with your balance."

"Right, I get that. But..."

"You know, pride goeth before the fall," Carson added. "And if you fall, you could break a bone. And then you would be laid up for even longer than this heart thing."

"I'll consider it." Jack let go of Andy's hand and Carson watched as his son hurried toward Kylie.

Every day they stayed meant another day of his children getting attached. They loved the ranch, their grandfather Jack, their uncle Isaac and they especially loved Kylie. She filled a place in their hearts that had been empty since they lost Anna.

"Come on," Isaac said, opening the door for Jack. "They've already started."

"Kylie, which pie did you bake?" Jack asked as they made their way through the crowded fellowship hall in search of an empty table.

Carson spotted one and pointed.

"Eve baked a couple of apple pies, but I also made a chocolate chess pie."

"My favorite," Jack said. "I hope we get that one. I want a piece of that for dessert."

"Jack, you're missing the point," Isaac said as they sat down. "The person who buys the pie gets to sit with the baker of the pie and enjoy it with them. They have picnic tables and blankets outside. You get the leftovers."

"I don't mind leftovers." Jack winked at Andy, and Carson watched his son smile, then reach to hug his dog.

The changes in his son were obvious. In the short time they'd been in Hope at Mercy Ranch, Andy had gained some independence. He smiled more. He talked more. Carson had known they needed to get out of Dallas. They had needed a change of scenery. But he hadn't thought what they needed was Mercy Ranch.

He still believed that Chicago would be beneficial to his family. Like Dallas, Chicago had more to offer than a small town like Hope. But even as those thoughts ran through his mind, his gaze scanned the table of people gathered with them and he knew that these people had been beneficial, as well.

It would be hard to leave this place. Very hard.

His gaze connected with Kylie's and she didn't smile. Her eyes, warm toffee, held his and asked unspoken questions. He had kissed her. He shouldn't havc, not now when he was close to leaving. Neither of them needed to deal with letting go.

The pie auction carried on, even though he hadn't been paying attention. He shifted in his seat to watch the goings-on. People around them were laughing, and a few good-natured arguments broke out as they bid on the best pies. In the first half of the auction, the pies were baked by ladies in the community, and husbands, brothers, fathers did all the bidding. Friendly bickering happened every now and then when someone decided a certain pie was worth fighting for.

The second half of the auction, meant to be fun and maybe a little romantic, featured pies baked by the single ladies in town. Men moved toward the table that held the pies, glancing over the names and types of pie. And then, because it probably gave them an advantage, they stayed close to the auctioneer.

When Eve's pie came up for bid, the battle was fierce. In the end a local rancher, a little younger than Carson, managed to win the pie. Eve shot Isaac a glacial look.

"You were supposed to bid on my pie," Eve muttered under her breath.

"Yeah well, Jaxon gave me a fifty spot to let him win. I wasn't gonna argue with him."

"I don't want to eat pie with Jaxon Barns. I don't want to *talk* to Jaxon Barns," Eve hissed.

"Sorry," Isaac said, not really seeming like he was sorry.

Jack leaned across the table. "Eve, honey, he might be full of himself, but he isn't always rude."

"He's rude to me. That's all that matters."

"I don't think he means it, honey," Kylie said as she stood up. Her hand dropped to Eve's shoulder. "I'll be back in a few minutes."

"I could take him out back and knock some sense into him if you want," Isaac offered with a grin. "Hey, Kylie, don't run off because they're about to auction your pie!"

She glared at him, then spun on her heel and left the room.

"That was uncalled for," Jack chastised. "You know she only did this to help the group home."

The bidding started and Isaac tossed a look Carson's way, challenging him to something. He wasn't sure what.

Carson considered going after Kylie but he knew that would stir up gossip. And then what would happen?

The bidding for Kylie's pie continued. Carson raised his hand, upping the amount by five dollars. Isaac grinned and doubled Carson's bid. People around them laughed and made comments about the West brothers feuding over Kylie.

Carson thought about letting Isaac win but when the auctioneer asked him if he was willing to bid thirty dollars, Carson raised the bid to thirty.

Isaac raised his hand and shouted out, "Fifty!"

"Boys, you'd best figure this one out," the auctioneer teased.

That's when Carson should have backed out, but Isaac arched a brow at him and tipped that cowboy hat back with a grin. The cinnamon toothpick stuck out of the corner of his mouth and he laughed.

"I'll let you win," Isaac said. "On one condition. You have to look at the clinic. You don't have to stay in Hope and be our doctor, but at least take a look, you stubborn fool."

Carson's hand went up one last time as the auctioneer cajoled, asking for a bid that would beat the fifty dollars from Isaac West. "One hundred dollars."

The crowd erupted in cheers and applause. Isaac sat back in his chair and laughed. Carson looked at him as the tray with pie and a thermos of coffee with cups was delivered to their table.

"Joke's on you, man. Eve is with Jaxon Barns and I'm gonna have pie with Kylie. That means you're on babysitting detail with these two."

Carson grinned as he stood and picked up the tray that had been set in front of him.

"You're definitely getting the better end of the deal," Isaac said. "If you can find Kylie."

"I can find her."

With more confidence than he felt, he walked off with the tray in search of his…date.

Dating wasn't something he'd done a lot of in recent years. Last year he'd gone out with a nurse from work and with a social worker. Both times he'd felt as if he had made the biggest mistake of his life.

He didn't want Kylie to be a mistake. He also didn't want to hurt her.

When he didn't find her inside the fellowship hall, he went out the side door and across the lawn. He spotted Eve with Jaxon Barns. Jaxon looked happy. Eve looked as if she'd be happier having a root canal. He headed in their direction.

"Have you seen Kylie?"

Eve pointed toward the creek at the back of the property.

"She headed that way."

"Was she okay?" he asked.

Eve looked puzzled. "Why wouldn't she be? Did you upset her?" She started to give him the stink eye.

"No, I didn't. But I did buy her pie in the auction. Don't worry, I'll find her."

He left them alone and started toward the creek, because he thought he knew where she might be going. If she guessed he would buy her pie, she'd probably head for the spot a good five-minute walk downstream. The place where they'd shared that first kiss.

Kylie couldn't say why she'd picked this spot exactly. She'd left the church needing a quiet place to think. She hadn't wanted to deal with all the hubbub surrounding the pie auction. She would have preferred donating money and staying at home. She didn't want to be bid on. She didn't want to sit with someone and pretend to care.

She didn't want to date. She didn't want to put on a fake smile, try to think of witty things to say, deal with the eventual good-night kiss or the awkward attempt to ask her on a second date. Or the even more awkward moment when they didn't ask for a second date.

Not that she had really dated. Not once in four years.

Figured that only one person could have her thinking of dating and of kisses. Carson West. Because of him, she was now sitting on the bank of the creek skipping rocks across the surface of the water.

"I can still do better than you," he said from across the creek.

She looked up and smiled in spite of herself. He stood on the opposite bank, a tray balanced in his right hand.

Early evening sun filtered through the leaves, capturing him in patches of golden light. A work of art. She smiled at the thought. Eve would have laughed.

He looked as if he belonged in Hope, with his jeans, boots and a button-up shirt with the sleeves rolled to the elbows. He had nice arms. What woman looked at a man like Carson and thought about his arms? But they were nice, so she wouldn't apologize.

"Are you going to invite me over?" he asked.

"Do you require an invitation? You bought the pie. That gives you all the invitation you need."

"I'll have you know I paid one hundred dollars for this pie," he called out, his voice competing with the sound of rushing of water over rocks.

"You shouldn't have. It's from a mix."

He lifted the tray and sniffed the pie. "I don't think so. It smells too good. What do you think, should I sit over here and eat by myself?"

"No, you most definitely shouldn't. You have to cross by the tree up there. There are a couple of places that are barely an inch deep."

He sat down, putting the tray on the grass next to him. She watched as he pulled off his boots, then his socks. Next he rolled up his jeans. He left his boots behind, picked up the tray and eased down the bank, stepping gingerly into the cold spring water.

"Oh wow, that's refreshing." He cringed a little and took a cautious step. "Ouch, ouch, ouch."

She laughed as he slowly made his way across the creek. "You should have left your boots on, cowboy."

"I paid a lot for those boots."

"Don't cut your feet on glass."

He paused, surveyed the ground and walked carefully in her direction. "First I had to outbid my brother. Second, I had to promise to look at the clinic. Third, I have to wade the creek, dodge glass *and* walk on rocks?"

"You know I'm worth it," she boasted, then wished she hadn't. "Well, maybe just the pie."

He tossed her the blanket he'd carried over his arm. "You're worth it, Kylie."

"Stop." She drew her knees up and hugged them to her. "You aren't supposed to be so charming. Don't make this complicated. It's just pie with an old friend."

"You're right," he agreed. "I don't want to make this complicated. I just want to sit down and have pie with a friend."

"Maybe this is good for us. We've both been through a lot and I have a feeling you've been as guarded as I have been. It's okay to open up and have friends." With each other, they could have a safe space. Someone who understood that the other person wasn't looking for commitments.

"I agree." He sighed. "The last few years, I've worked. I've taken care of my children. We stopped going to church. We rarely see family. The nanny would take them to the park or play dates. But mostly we've been in a bubble."

"And I broke the bubble?" she asked. The words just slipped out and she worried she might be giving herself too much credit.

But he leaned toward her. He didn't kiss her but he gave her a bite of the rich chocolate chess pie. She closed her mouth over the fork and shut her eyes because she couldn't eat that pie and look into gray eyes that saw too much. Made her feel too much.

When she opened her eyes, he pulled back the fork and leaned in to kiss the corner of her mouth. Her heart did a dance in her chest. She reminded herself that they were friends. Just friends. It was easy enough. He got her. He knew what she'd been through.

He pulled away from her, smiled and took a bite of pie. “It really is good.”

“Thank you. It isn’t from a box.”

“I know.” He scooped a slice of pie onto a paper plate and handed it to her. And then he picked up the pie pan and started to devour what was left.

“You’re going to eat the entire pie?”

He glanced up. “I gave you a slice. This was a very expensive pie. You’re a very expensive date.”

She drew back a little.

“It’s not a date,” she corrected him. “You bought my pie, so you’re stuck with me.”

“I’m not stuck with you. I could have let Isaac win the bidding. I chose not to.”

“Because you don’t like to lose.”

He grinned, his eyes crinkling at the corners. “You’re right. I don’t.”

“Who’s watching Maggie and Andy?” She needed to change the subject.

“Jack and Isaac.”

She cringed. “Really? You left them with two grown men who are more like children than your kids?”

“I trust them,” he said. “And if all else fails, they have Rambo with them.”

She found herself smiling as they ate their pie in companionable silence. Crickets sang as the sun sank on the western horizon and birds swooped through the branches of the tree as they prepared to roost.

"We should go." She put a hand on his shoulder and stood.

He looked up at her. "Yes, probably. But this was nice. I'm glad we had this. It means a lot to me."

She felt the corners of her mouth tug up. "It was nice. But you know this can't happen again. Right?"

"Of course. But friendship is good though."

"I'm not looking for a relationship but I'm glad we can be friends."

He laughed as he got to his feet and gathered up the dishes and the tray. She picked up the blanket. He looked at her, into her eyes, then leaned over to kiss her cheek. It was sweet. It was the kiss of a friend.

Which was exactly what she wanted. Nothing more. A friend was someone you could say goodbye to without it feeling like a broken heart. A woman could promise to call a friend. Friends sent cards and got together once in a while when they were in the same town.

Friendships were safe.

That's what she wanted, needed. Safe. Wasn't it?

Chapter Fourteen

"So, how was the pie the other day?" Isaac asked as he and Carson pulled up to the clinic Jack had had built.

It wasn't much of a clinic. It was just a metal building with a gravel parking lot located on the edge of town. They got out of the truck and headed for the side door.

"The pie was good," Carson said, shooting his brother a look, wondering where this line of questioning would lead them.

"Kylie?"

"Is a good cook," he answered, knowing that wasn't what Isaac wanted from him. It was still difficult to think of the stranger walking next to him as his brother. They had the same hair, the same eyes, the same height, but so did a lot of other people. The two of them just happened to share the same DNA.

They stepped inside and Isaac flipped on the lights.

It looked like the standard small-town facility. A waiting room, office, several exam rooms. Carson went from room to room and admitted silently to himself that Jack had done something decent here. A family practitioner would have a decent start in Hope.

"Yeah, she's a decent cook. She's more than a decent person."

Carson got it. This was a warning. "You don't have to tell me what kind of person she is. If you're warning me not to hurt her, I think Kylie and I both know where we stand."

"Your kids love her."

Yeah, his kids did love her. That had been his concern from the beginning. They were drawn to her. They wanted—needed—a mom. Sure, they had him, but he wasn't soft, maternal, and he didn't bake cookies. He could put a bandage on a scrape but making it feel better with a hug wasn't his strong suit.

"This is a nice facility." Changing the subject seemed to be the best course of action.

"Nice?" Isaac asked as they walked through the building.

"Better than nice. He did a good job with this. Wish I'd known he had all of this money when we were kids and wearing holes in our shoes."

"He says he wasn't in any condition to have access to it back in the day, so he had a lawyer keep most of it tied up. But what he could get his hands on, he blew through. Bought horses, gambled, paid my mother off."

"I guess we lived the same life in different places."

Isaac stopped and leaned his shoulder against the wall. "Yeah, I guess. We weren't that far away. Surprised we never bumped into each other. We lived on the other side of Grove."

Isaac headed down the hall, to a back office.

Carson watched the other man closely. From time to time Isaac would touch the wall, as if to balance himself. He also always kept Carson on his right side. He'd noticed this before, but it was becoming clearer what the problems were.

"I guess there's no chance you'll stay?" Isaac asked as they left the building.

"I can't."

"Can't or won't?" Isaac pulled his keys out of his pocket and tossed them to Carson. "Drive?"

Carson looked at the keys and then at Isaac. "You okay? I know you don't want me to pry."

"No, I don't. If I was fine, would I be letting you drive?"

"Guess you wouldn't. Fair enough. But if you need anything…" He left the offer hanging.

"You won't be here, so what's the point. I'll

find a doctor around these parts." Isaac got in on the passenger side and leaned his seat back.

"Where to?"

"Feed store." Isaac reached for sunglasses and slipped them on.

"Got it." Carson eased the truck onto the main road.

The feed store sat next to the train tracks, because that's the way it used to be done. Local people brought in their grains, the trains loaded them or unloaded other products. He'd been told that most of that had changed back in the 1970s. But the feed store still stood, handling produce and grains for locals, but not shipping anything across the country as they had once done.

"Do you want to stay in the truck?" he asked Isaac as they sat in the parked truck.

"Yeah, I think I will." Isaac pulled his hat down over his face. "If anyone asks, I've got the flu. It's contagious so they shouldn't get close."

Carson gave him another careful look and headed into the feed store. He remembered going there a lot as a kid. He would ride to town with Jack, have breakfast at Mattie's and then hit the feed store and the grocery store. At the feed store there were always a few locals sitting around drinking coffee and talking about the price of cattle, milk and horses and the possibility of rain.

Life in Hope hadn't been all bad. Lots of memories were bubbling up, after having been pushed aside for a lot of years.

Walking through the door was a lot like stepping back in time. He could almost imagine he was a kid again. He'd get a bottle of grape soda from the cooler and a candy stick out of the canister on the counter. The store smelled the same, too. Molasses used in grain, the chemical smell of bug spray, and coffee that had been too long on the burner. He headed to the counter and smiled when he realized that it was the same woman who had been there twenty years ago.

"Well, look who's here—it's Carson West. Last time I saw you, you were a skinny little boy who hadn't hit his growth spurt. Skinny and brown as a nut from being out in the sun all day. Look at you now. I heard you're a big surgeon in Dallas. Your daddy is so proud of you." She finally took a breath. Before she could ramble on some more, he had to say something.

Finally, he remembered her name. "It's good to see you, Mrs. Baxter."

"How does it feel to be back at the ranch? Things have changed, haven't they?"

"Yes, things have definitely changed." He leaned back and checked the truck and Isaac. "I need to place an order. Isaac has the flu so he sent me in to tell you all to deliver the regular order of grain tomorrow and he needs a few mineral blocks."

"I can do that." She wrote down the order on a notepad. "Now, I sure hope you're planning on staying in town. That new clinic sure could use a doctor."

"Yes, it is a nice clinic. And I'm sure they'll find someone to work there."

Her features fell in disappointment. "Oh, I see. You won't be staying, then?"

"I'm afraid not. I have plans to move to Chicago."

"Well, I hope you don't mind me saying, you sure look like you belong in Hope," she said with a smile that didn't quite reach her eyes. "But then, I guess it would be difficult for you to come back here after having such an amazing career."

"I'm just getting started on that career."

"Oh, of course, but you've done really well for yourself."

He peeked again at the truck. "Well, it was good catching up with you. I should go. Isaac is pretty sick."

"He gets a little peaked from time to time. I hope it's nothing serious."

"Nah, he's fine."

Carson headed to the truck. He climbed back behind the wheel and glanced at his brother.

Isaac shifted and pushed his hat up enough that Carson could see his eyes.

"Did Marla put you through the mill with a million questions?"

"She barely took a breath."

Isaac pulled the hat back down over his eyes. "She means well but the woman knows everything about everyone in the three-state area."

By that he meant Oklahoma, Missouri and Arkansas. Carson grinned as he backed out of the parking space. "She tried to get as much information out of me as humanly possible in the five minutes I was in there."

When they pulled into the garage of the main house, Isaac pushed his hat back and raised the seat. He swiped at the perspiration on his brow.

"You okay?"

"I will be," he grumbled as he slowly got out of the truck.

"I could take you to the ER," Carson offered.

"I don't need the ER."

"Fine, but do you have something for the pain?"

Isaac made an attempt at shoving past him. "I can only have over-the-counter pain meds."

Carson knew what that meant, and sighed.

Isaac stopped on the steps to the house and pulled the cinnamon toothpick out of his mouth. "My binkie."

"Yeah, I get it. I'm sorry."

"You don't have to get all sympathetic and big brother protector. It happens. You come home injured and you have no other options but pain meds. And then you realize the pain is still there and the meds aren't working. You don't want to be an addict, but you also don't want to live in pain. And then the addiction has you. I'm on the other side and I'm a winner. No need for sympathy."

Carson held his hands up in surrender. "Wouldn't think of it."

Isaac pushed the door open. "I'm going inside for some tea."

"Tea?" Carson followed him through the utility room.

"Feverfew, lavender and mint," he listed as he walked to the kitchen. "It might be a placebo but it helps."

"I don't doubt it works."

Isaac leaned on the counter and took a deep breath. Kylie appeared from the family room, Andy and Maggie following her. He'd left his children with Jack. He gave her a questioning look and dropped his gaze from her to his children.

"Jack had to go out to the barn. Problem with some cattle he had delivered today. Don't worry, they're fine." Kylie switched her focus to Isaac. "Need tea?"

"This stinks," Isaac muttered as he sat on a stool.

Kylie put a teapot on the stove and leaned down to pick up Maggie. Carson watched as his daughter snuggled close to Kylie.

"I should take her," he said. "They need a nap and I know you have other things to do."

"Carson, I don't mind." Kylie dropped a kiss on his daughter's head.

Of course she didn't, but he saw a bond forming when he looked at the two of them. He saw heartache when they left—not just his children, but Kylie. He ignored other thoughts that were popping into his head that he didn't want to acknowledge. He had to leave soon. That was the harsh reality. But he wasn't sure that he wanted to. That was the even harsher truth.

Kylie had never had a difficult time letting go. She'd done it enough times in her life that she should be a pro at it. But releasing Maggie to Carson, that took something from her. If he hadn't been looking at her with that expression of concern, as if he thought she might fall apart, maybe she wouldn't feel so wounded.

He had gotten the diagnosis correct, though. She thought she might fall apart. When he put the children back in that SUV and they drove away for good, she knew it would hurt worse than anything she'd ever experienced.

She definitely wasn't looking forward to it.

Carson held Maggie and reached a hand out for Andy. "How about if I read you a story? Andy can help us."

Kylie turned away. She couldn't watch. Carson would see the longing in her eyes. He would feel sorry for her. She didn't want sympathy. Or pity.

The teapot began to whistle. She poured the water in the cup and the aroma, bitter but soothing, filled the air. She wanted to stand and breathe in the lavender until her heart calmed down a bit.

"Kylie?" Isaac reached a hand across the counter. "You okay?"

"Of course."

"Make yourself a cup, why don't you," he suggested.

She shook her head. She squeezed a bit of honey in the tea and stirred. Carefully she slid it across the counter to him.

"Sit with me," he prodded. His tone was brotherly and it shattered her calm.

She shook her head. "No, I think I have to go for a walk."

"I'm going to hurt him," Isaac muttered, pushing himself up from the stool.

"It isn't his fault." She brushed at dampness in her eyes. "I need to go now."

Kylie walked out the back door and took a deep breath. She loved October. And this was perfect weather. The air was cooler than it had been for several days. She stepped down off the patio and headed for the corral where a few horses moved about, reaching occasionally for grass. One of the horses, a pale, almost white palomino saw her and trotted up to the fence. She'd seen him yesterday when they unloaded the new horses. He had stood out to her. She'd immediately asked Jack what he had planned for the animal.

Jack had told her he was just extra stock for the ranch, for the group home, wherever they needed him. Or for her, if that's what she wanted, he said. She rubbed the horse's face as he reached across the white vinyl rail of the fence.

"Look at you, like moonlight."

The horse moved his head up and down as if he understood the compliment. "You like that, do you?"

She leaned close, inhaling his scent. She loved the smell of horses when they were warm from the sun.

Footsteps crunching on the gravel warned that she was no longer alone. She glanced back, surprised to see Carson. She really hadn't wanted him to follow her. It only made things more difficult, having him feel as if he needed to check on her, comfort her. And she could see in his eyes that was what he planned.

She really didn't need to be coddled. She'd been strong all of her life. She wasn't used to needing anyone, or to leaning on someone. She didn't want to be a person he felt he had to take care of. She didn't want to look in his eyes and see that he still held back because he hadn't let go of Anna. And she didn't like that she felt that way.

"Are you okay?" he asked as he stood next to her at the fence. The horse reached, nipping a little at his sleeve. He ran his hand down the horse's neck. "Nice horse."

"He is. Jack told me I could claim him. I don't see a reason to. I'm just going to pet him, talk to him and love him. Someone else can ride him."

"You could ride him."

"I don't think I can." She kissed the horse on the nose. "Where are the kids?"

"Sleeping on a pallet on the floor. Rambo is next to Andy. Jack is in his recliner. Isaac is stretched out on the sofa watching old episodes of *Cops*. I have full confidence that between the two grown men and the dog, my children are safe."

"I'm sure they are."

He paused for a moment. Then he murmured, "They'll miss you, you know."

She blinked, his words hitting somewhere near her heart the way an arrow would penetrate the most vulnerable area. She would miss his children. She would miss him.

"I'll miss them, too," she admitted. "I knew it the day you drove up that this would be difficult. I knew if you stayed more than an hour that I would want you to stay forever. That I would want them to stay. I realize I shouldn't feel this way about someone I really barely know. But life is funny that way."

"We were friends once. That isn't barely knowing someone. We shared a lot of secrets, you and me."

She hid her face, thinking of some of those most painful secrets she'd told him. Things that no child should have had to confide to a friend. She should have had a parent to turn to.

"Yes, we were friends," she admitted.

He slid an arm around her waist and pulled her close. "If things had been different…"

They might have been high school sweethearts, she thought. They might have gotten married. She shook off that old dream. If he had stayed here, Andy or Maggie wouldn't exist.

She eased herself from his embrace. "I can't have children."

"What?" His voice changed, subtly to a softer tone, the way people talked to someone who they thought might fall apart.

She wasn't going to fall apart. His children had taught her something. They'd taught her she could love a child completely, a child that wasn't hers. Maybe that wasn't the case for everyone, but it seemed to be true for her.

"The shrapnel did damage to my legs, my hips, and it did some internal damage." She reached for the horse again, needing to touch something real, living.

"I'm so sorry, Kylie." His arm tightened around her.

"Please don't. It's just, I'm telling you this so you know I have so much to be thankful for. I love my life on this ranch. I love helping others. Please don't mess that up."

By making her want more. By making her want him, and children with him. His children.

She walked away, and she wasn't surprised that he let her go. Either he didn't want to have this conversation. Or he knew she needed space. Either way, he let her go.

She wished he'd come after her. A small, selfish part of her wanted him to chase after her and tell her they could be more than friends. He could share his life and his children with her. He could settle for Hope, settle for being a small-town doctor.

But the truth was, why would he want to settle? Settle for someone broken who couldn't have children? Settle for something small when he could go somewhere big and be something amazing?

It seemed cruel, that after all these years, he had dropped back in her life for just a temporary visit. A visit that showed her what she'd missed out on.

She almost wished he'd never come back at all.

Almost.

Chapter Fifteen

"When do you plan on leaving?" Jack asked on Sunday morning.

Carson poured his dad a cup of coffee. "About two weeks ago."

Jack sipped his coffee, a guilty grin on his face. "Yeah, I guess we did change your plans."

"Yeah, you did." Carson grabbed up their dirty plates and put them in the dishwasher. The kids had eaten and were in the family room watching television, already dressed for church. "I have to leave Tuesday."

"I see. Well, it was a good visit. And I hope you can come back for a visit," Jack said lightly, a little too easily.

"It'll depend on the job situation."

"You're sure you want to leave?"

"I have to."

Jack cocked his head to the side and studied

him. "There's a mighty big difference between *have* to and *want* to."

Carson realized his mistake. One word changed everything.

"I *have* to," he repeated. He no longer really knew his reasons why. He could think of a few. He'd made a commitment, a plan, and he always stuck to his plans. That's how he'd gotten where he was. He was a trauma surgeon, not a family practitioner. And Andy. Now, with the dog, things had changed. There would be opportunities that hadn't been there before. But leaving wouldn't be easy. The time spent at Mercy Ranch had changed them all.

"What about Kylie?" Jack asked, his voice softer, less gruff.

"Kylie is amazing and I'm glad she's here. But we're just friends."

"Really? Is that what you kids call it now? Friends?"

Carson didn't know what to call it. He knew that Kylie had put up a wall between them. Probably to protect herself. That's about the only thing he knew, other than that when he had kissed her he'd felt a lot of things, including feelings of guilt.

"Carson, do you know why I never remarried?"

"Nope, but I guess you're going to tell me."

Jack chuckled and got up to pour himself another cup of coffee. He sat back down and pointed to the empty stool next to him. Carson remained standing.

"I never felt divorced. Your mother left so quickly and without a goodbye. It never seemed real. I kept thinking she would come back one day."

"Stop." Carson walked away. "I'm not doing this with you."

"I know, but you're going to have to think about what I'm saying, because if you don't, you're going to miss out on something. Your kids will miss out. You're determined to get to Chicago and start a new life for yourself and your kids, but you haven't dealt with your old life."

"Okay, you've said what you wanted to say. Let's just leave it there. If and when I ever decide to move on, it's going to be my decision. *Mine.* No one else's."

He hadn't heard the door open but he saw her. Kylie stood just inside the back door, her face pale. "I'm sorry, I didn't mean to intrude. I should knock once in a while."

"Don't be ridiculous. You've never knocked and you're not going to start now." Jack waved her forward. "Get a cup of coffee, and there's some left of the healthy breakfast Carson made."

"Thanks, I already ate."

"I bet it wasn't tofu." Jack made a face, obviously trying to lighten the mood, but when he looked at Kylie, Carson saw her emotions written plainly on her face. He felt the same but knew better than to mention it to her. She'd made it clear that she needed to be strong.

"Don't make fun, Jack. You ate everything on your plate," Carson said, defending his breakfast. His eyes lingered on Kylie and the hurt look on her face.

She had made it pretty clear she wasn't interested in a relationship, but here they were, dancing around each other, hurting each other.

"Do you want to ride to church with us?" Jack asked her. She looked unsure. Then she nodded.

"If you don't mind. Eve is staying home today. She's a little under the weather."

Carson looked up at that. "Anything I can do to help?"

Kylie shook her head. "Not really. She didn't sleep well last night. Spasms."

"Does she need some of that tea of yours?" Jack asked. "I drank some last night and slept better than I have in ages."

"She isn't a big fan, but I got her to drink some this morning."

"More teas?" Carson asked.

Kylie looked at him then and he saw that her

eyes were dark rimmed. She hadn't slept well either. He wanted to mention it but she had that closed-off air about her. She wouldn't welcome him prying into her life or her sleeping habits.

"We try different herbal teas for the people who can't take pain meds or other prescriptions," she explained.

"Yes, I remember the one you gave Isaac. Speaking of Isaac, where is he?"

"Went to church early. I need to finish getting ready." Jack slid off the stool and took a moment to get his balance.

Carson stood close by, just in case.

"I'm going to get my photo albums," Jack continued as he walked away. "Today you need to look at them. I want you to see what I saw in your life, as a bystander."

"I don't need to see the photos. I lived it, remember?"

Jack got to the door and glanced back. "I thought Maggie and Andy would like to see."

Carson shifted his attention to Kylie. "Did you put him up to this?"

"Of course not," she said. "You should know me better than that."

He did, of course.

"You're right and I'm sorry."

"You're forgiven." She headed to the family room where Maggie and Andy were playing.

Carson stood in the doorway watching her interact with them, watching them get more and more attached to her. She hugged Maggie, started to tickle Andy but pulled back when he stiffened. She understood them. All three of them. And he understood her. She was trying to hold on to the happiness she'd found here on the ranch.

Jack appeared. He stood next to Carson, watching the scene in front of them. After a few minutes he put a hand on Carson's shoulder and squeezed.

"We should get to church," he said.

Carson nodded. "Kids, time to go."

When they got to church, the parking lot was crowded. People milled about; others were going up the front steps. Carson found a parking space, and they all got out and started walking toward the church together. Isaac met up with them as they walked through the door.

Isaac grinned. "The whole family going to church. Even the black sheep doctor."

"There are days I don't care much for you." Carson scowled as they slid into a pew and sat down.

"Yeah, well, the feeling's mutual, man." Isaac

picked up Maggie and placed her on his knee. He bounced and she yelled, "Yeehaw!"

"Not in church, sweetie," Carson warned.

"He takes all of the fun out of things," Isaac whispered in Maggie's ear. But he stopped bouncing his knee.

As much as Isaac aggravated him, Carson liked him. It would take some time to get used to the fact that they were brothers. But he could definitely see them having some sort of relationship.

Fortunately church started and he didn't have to think too deeply about this family, the ranch and leaving. Instead he had to think about the words of the pastor as he talked about contentment. About settling in to the place where God wants us and realizing there is a purpose for being there. It might not have been our plan, or our first or even fourth choice, but if it is God's choice, if we give it time, we find contentment. Out of the corner of his eye he saw Kylie wipe a tear from her cheek.

Kylie hadn't planned on being a part of looking over Jack's memory books. She'd helped him put the books together with all the photos he'd taken through the years, all the newspaper clippings he'd cut out and the school papers that had been sent to him. And yet here she was, watching as Jack directed Isaac to get the tub of photo albums and bring them to the living room.

Her heart ached, knowing this trip down memory lane wouldn't be easy for any of them. Her gaze lingered on Andy. It would be most difficult for him. Carson knew it, too. He'd been watching his son, monitoring his behavior, his mood.

She wanted to distance herself because she knew how much she'd miss them when they left. She knew how much she'd missed Carson the first time he went away. Her fragile teen heart had been so broken at his disappearance. But now, knowing how it felt to have him here, sharing her days, she was worried she wouldn't survive it.

She shook her head, wishing she could tell him the truth. But the thought of making him stay out of guilt? No way.

Isaac returned with the tub and removed the lid. His normal carefree smile had disappeared. He glanced down at his niece and nephew, and Kylie thought she saw a glimmer of protectiveness.

"I don't know about this," he said simply as he walked away.

Carson hugged his kids. "We're good. I bet there are pictures of me from high school. I probably look pretty bad. Maybe like Uncle Isaac."

Maggie laughed and he tickled her. "Andy, do you want to see a picture of me playing basketball?"

Andy nodded but his hands were buried in Rambo's fur. Kylie noticed that Isaac had decided to stay. He plopped down in the rocking chair in the far corner of the room. Jack sat in his recliner, his face pale as he studied his grandchildren.

"We don't have to do this," Jack backpedaled. Kylie gave him a sympathetic look.

"We're doing this, Jack," Carson said. "We're starting right here at the top."

He smiled. Kylie remembered the first picture in the first album. It was a photograph of the three West kids on horses, before they'd left the ranch. But later in the books were snapshots of their lives in Dallas. Sports, graduations, first days of college. They'd never known that Jack was there, driving all the way to Texas to witness those events.

And if he couldn't manage to attend, their mother had sent him photos.

The laughter and conversation stopped when he got to the final photo album. Wedding pictures of Carson and Anna, baby photos of Maggie and Andy. Kylie knew the pictures well. She'd placed each one in the album, watching the story of his life unfold. She'd been happy for him.

But now, she just couldn't let herself take the small pieces of him that remained. She wanted him whole. And wholly hers.

Carson flipped through the album and his expression shut down. He finally opened the book wide and allowed Maggie and Andy to see what was inside. Photos of an engagement, a happy couple, a wedding and then babies.

Andy shook his head and looked away.

Carson sighed. "Andy?"

Andy glanced back at the book. "Mommy."

"Yes, it's Mommy. She loved you very much."

As he spoke, Maggie jabbered, not understanding. She eventually slid free from his arms and toddled across the room to crawl into Kylie's lap. Kylie held her close.

"Mommy," Maggie whispered.

Kylie's heart shattered. She wanted to put Maggie down and run from the room. But instead she looked up, met Carson's steady gaze, saw the pain as he held his son and processed what his daughter had said.

Isaac got up quickly, leaving the rocking chair banging against the wall. "I've got work to do."

Kylie let her eyes drop to Andy. He had taken the book from Carson and flipped through the pages. And on each page he would point to his mother. It was a painful thing to watch but there was something amazing about it, too. As Andy looked at the photos, he smiled a little, as if he'd needed the images to restore the good memories. He started to tap his hand against his leg, and Rambo did what they'd trained him to do. He reached over and nudged Andy's hand, stopping the motion. Andy patted the dog's head, not even aware that the dog had stopped his behavior.

Carson noticed, as well. He reached out to pet the dog and told him he was a good boy.

Kylie couldn't be sad. Not as she watched them in that moment. She knew that they'd be fine. She knew they would settle somewhere, Carson would get an amazing job, and they'd be happy again.

She stood, knowing it was time for her to walk away from this. She settled Maggie back in her daddy's lap and kissed Andy on the head.

"Where are you going?" Carson asked.

"I have work to do." She glanced at the pictures Andy perused and felt a tiny hint of sadness. But not so much she couldn't deal with it.

Seeing Andy happy meant everything.

"You don't have to go," Carson told her.

"I do, actually," she said.

He stood up, leaving Andy with the photo album.

"I'll walk you out."

"I wish you wouldn't."

He didn't listen to her.

She studied his handsome face, wishing she'd been more than the girl he'd quickly forgotten. Yes, they'd just been kids. But what she'd felt for him had nothing to do with puppy love. She loved him deep down, completely.

They walked to the back door.

"I don't want to leave with this between us," Carson said as they stood on the patio.

She couldn't look at him, standing there. This was not the boy she'd once known. He was a man now, in his jeans and boots, his lean stubbled cheeks. She looked her fill. Because he was leaving.

"At least this time we get to say goodbye."

"I'll be back," he told her. "I told Jack we would try to come back for a visit. And I'll be here for his surgery."

"I know you'll be back," she said. She tried to say more, but stopped herself. She needed a moment to gather her thoughts. She had to say this. For herself. "Carson, I'm happy here. I love this ranch, the people, and most of the time, I love myself."

His hand reached for hers.

She pulled her hand back. "No, don't do that. When you come back, we have to keep boundaries in place. Because I love you, Carson. I love you so much it hurts. Maybe when we were kids it was puppy love or a teenage crush, or whatever people call it. But I have loved you my whole life. And you forgot me. You forgot that you promised to marry me. You forgot that you told me you loved me. I'm trying hard not to be hurt by that, but it does hurt. So this ends. The hand holding, the kisses, the soft looks. I'm not settling for the pieces of you she left behind."

"I'm not giving you pieces."

"I know," she said softly. "You're giving me nothing."

"I let her down in the worst way imaginable."

Her heart broke, shattered a little. "You know in your heart it wasn't your fault. It was the fault of the drunk driver who crossed the road. You were all victims that day. Anna, you, your children."

"It was my fault." He briefly closed his eyes. "She asked me to go to the store. I was too busy."

"You weren't the driver who hit her. You know that. You did what any of us might have done. You told her you couldn't go. It wasn't your fault."

"But it sure feels that way. And I'll do everything in my power to keep my kids safe and to do what's best for them."

Even leaving, she realized. Leaving her.

She felt for him, but she didn't touch him, didn't offer him her hand. Because even though he'd given her the truth, he still couldn't give her his heart.

And selfish as it might seem, she wanted all of him.

She wanted all or nothing.

Chapter Sixteen

Carson loaded the SUV as Jack sat on the patio watching. He had to admit, he was torn. He knew Kylie had made a good point. She deserved everything. She especially deserved a heart that was whole. But at this point, he didn't know what he was feeling.

Isaac came out of the house with a smaller suitcase. When he got close, he tossed it to Carson. The suitcase let out a yowl. He looked from the canvas bag to his brother.

"What in the world is in this thing?"

Isaac grinned. "Maggie packed it."

"So you're going to tell me you don't know what is in here? Because I didn't watch her pack it, but from the gentle way you tossed it at my head, and the noises coming from inside, I'm sure I don't want this in my truck."

Isaac poked the brim of his hat, pushing it back a bit. "You take all of the fun out of life."

He guessed maybe he did, a little. He'd always been the older brother, the studious brother, the protector. "Even if I wanted a cat, we can't take one across the country in a suitcase."

Maggie toddled out of the house with Andy and Rambo. Andy looked at the suitcases and at Carson. "No."

"Andy, we have to." Carson knelt in front of his son. "We talked about this last night. We have to go to Chicago. We'll find a house with a yard. Maybe we'll even get a cat. And in a few weeks we'll come back here to visit."

"I want Kylie," Maggie cried, rubbing at her eyes with her fists. Her hair had been pulled up in short pigtails. Isaac must have done that because the tails were pointed in two directions and random hairs were loose and curling in all directions.

"Kylie said goodbye to us last night." He hugged Maggie and then Andy. "Come on, we have to go let that cat loose in the barn. We can't take him away from his cat family."

The words weren't lost on him. He was taking his children away from family. He hadn't planned it this way, that they'd develop family ties here.

The suitcase jumped in his arms. He could

hear Jack and Isaac laughing. He shot them dirty looks. "The two of you could help."

Jack shrugged. "We're helping. We're showing you how much you'll miss this."

He took Maggie by the hand and handled the suitcase with care. "Come on, Andy."

"And Rambo," Maggie insisted.

"Yes, and Rambo. We can't take a cat but we can take the dog."

He glanced toward Kylie's apartment. Her car was gone. She'd left for the day. She didn't want sad goodbyes. She didn't want to watch them drive away. She'd told him last night that she planned on taking a day trip today.

When they got to the stable, he set the suitcase on the ground near the food and water bowls for the barn cats. He glanced at Maggie and Andy. Both were watching; neither was very happy.

"I want a kitty." Maggie frowned at the suitcase.

"How did you get this one in the suitcase?" Carson asked.

"Uncle Isaac," Andy replied.

He figured that Isaac had something to do with this. Carson bit back a smile as he unzipped the bag. The kitten had curled up in a corner with a handful of cat food. When it saw light, it hissed and jumped out to freedom. The cat obviously didn't want to relocate to the city.

Carson smiled at Maggie. "The cat likes living here. When we come back to visit, we can see him."

"Andy, Daddy." She pointed to the door.

Andy had already disappeared. But he had Rambo. Carson picked up his daughter and the now empty suitcase and went after his son. He found him quickly. Andy and Rambo were in the yard. Andy was trying to walk away but Rambo was circling him the way a border collie circled cattle.

"Good boy, Rambo." Carson gave the dog one of the treats he kept in a bag in his pocket.

"I don't want to go." Andy looked up at him, tears shimmering in his gray eyes.

"I know you don't, Andy. But this isn't our home. It's Grandpa's home. It's Isaac's home. But we're going to have a new home in Chicago. It's a city like Dallas."

"I want to stay here." Andy dropped to the ground. He started to tap his legs. The old behaviors still existed. But Rambo moved in, nudging his head under Andy's hands and forcing the boy to pet him.

"We can't stay." He picked Andy up and carried him the short distance back to the house.

Rambo followed. Maggie raced ahead of them, climbing the steps and piling onto Jack's lap.

"Time to go?" Jack said.

"Yeah, time to go." Carson carried Andy but he knew Maggie wouldn't willingly leave Jack. He looked to Isaac for help . "If you can bring Maggie?"

Isaac carried her. Jack walked along behind them, looking a lot sadder than the last time Carson had left this ranch. He remembered that Jack had been in a rage, throwing things. He'd told them to never come back. So they hadn't. Until now. And Carson thought back to the day he showed up here and what-all he'd wanted to say. He'd never said any of it.

"We'll be back," he repeated to Andy as he buckled him in his seat. "Rambo, get in."

Rambo jumped in the seat next to Andy and placed his head on Carson's son's arm. As if he knew this moment required special attention. The Lab's big yellow head leaned close and Andy placed his head on the dog's head.

Jack and Kylie had done this for them. They'd changed Andy's life. He closed the door and walked to the driver's side where Isaac was buckling Maggie in while Jack leaned on the door and told her something about ponies.

"Jack, I came here to tell you a lot of things," Carson started.

Isaac shot him a warning look. But he didn't stop.

"I came here to say a lot of things." Carson ignored Isaac. "But what I want to say most is thank you."

Jack stepped forward and hugged him, tight. "Mercy. I don't deserve it. But thank you."

"You deserve it, Jack. You do deserve it. I don't."

Carson hadn't thought of it before. Mercy. Forgiveness for someone not deserving. He couldn't even forgive himself let alone ask anyone else to forgive him.

"No one deserves it, Carson. That's the key to mercy. It is undeserved. I'm not sure what you're carrying around, but you need to find some forgiveness for yourself before it eats away at your soul. You're going to miss out."

By missing out he guessed Jack meant Kylie. But Kylie deserved more. She insisted she was happy with her life here. He wanted her to have more.

"I'll think about it." He hugged Jack one last time. "I'll be back in a couple of weeks."

"You'd better."

Isaac gave him a quick man hug. “You’re okay for a bossy older brother.”

Carson drove away a few minutes later. It was early morning and the sun was shining into the back seat. His kids were having a conversation about leaving and about Kylie and Jack and Isaac. Maggie did most of the talking but Andy added a word or two from time to time.

Mercy Ranch changed lives. It had changed theirs.

As he drove through town, he saw Kylie’s car at Mattie’s Café. He thought she was probably having a milkshake and curly fries.

He considered stopping and asking her if she would ever consider a man whose heart was on the mend. He wasn’t quite whole but he was getting there. He kept on driving.

She claimed she was happy with her life. And he wasn’t going to offer her anything less than his whole heart.

Kylie watched Carson’s SUV slow down, then keep going. Her heart had skipped a beat or two when she saw his brake lights. She’d thought maybe, just maybe.

“Do you need anything else?” Holly asked. The café was empty. It wasn’t breakfast or lunch. Even the gossip club had gone on back to their farms to take care of chores.

"No, I'm going to pay and head back to the house." She started to get up but Holly sat down.

They'd known each other as kids, although Holly was a few years younger. "They're hard men, the Wests."

The comment surprised Kylie. "Yes, I guess they are. You were the same age as Colt. I guess you were in school together?"

Holly grinned. "Yeah, we were. He was mean. A bully. But then he grew out of it."

"How do you know that?"

Holly arched a brow. "He's been through town a time or two. He checks on Jack."

"Jack has never said anything to me about Colt visiting."

"Jack doesn't know it." Holly patted her hand in an awkward attempt at offering comfort. "There's a lot Jack doesn't know. But it's been about five years since the last time Colt was in town. We had a falling-out. Anyway, they're hard to understand. And Carson is like one of those troubled romance heroes. He's in love with you but he won't let himself love you because he feels guilty. Maybe he feels like he's cheating on his wife by loving someone else."

"Yes, maybe." Kylie put money on the table. "Thanks, Holly."

Holly handed her the money. "My treat."

"Holly, how long have you owned the café?"

Holly turned a little pink. "Five years. When Mattie put it up for sale, I was able to come up with a down payment to buy the place."

"Maybe Jack knows more than you think." With that Kylie left and she heard Holly chuckle as the door closed behind her.

When she got back to the ranch, Jack was sitting on the patio with a book and a cup of coffee. She sat down next to him.

"They're gone." Jack looked up, his reading glasses perched on his nose. "I worry."

"About?"

"What if there is a time they come to visit and I don't remember them."

"You should have told him your fears, Jack. He would have understood. But we've talked about this. It could take years for you to develop the dementia associated with Parkinson's. Or it might not happen at all."

"Getting old is going to happen." He looked back at his book. "The same as night is going to happen, and the same as tomorrow is the day after today."

"You have a point. And we're all going to get somewhat forgetful."

"I don't want to forget my kids, or the family I have on this ranch. Or you."

"I won't let you. We'll start more memory

books. Maybe one of the ranch. We'll take photos of the rodeo coming up."

"That's a good idea. And I've contacted a lawyer."

"Why?"

She poured herself a cup of coffee from the thermos on the table. Jack took off his reading glasses and folded them. His left hand made the task difficult.

"I want to know that there's a trust, for the ranch, for my family, for you. I want it protected. Sometimes I think I've spent my whole life trying to protect this place. I got married to protect it. I got sober to protect it."

"Here's a thought. You could relax and just enjoy it," she joked with him.

"I'm enjoying it. I'd enjoy it more if we could get your smile back."

"I'll get my smile back," she promised. She stared into the coffee cup. "I'm happy here, Jack. That's the story, my story. And Carson has to find his happiness. I think he's close. I think being here on the ranch with you helped him. Maybe when he gets to Chicago he'll finally find peace."

Jack patted her hand. "It wasn't me or the ranch that helped him find anything. It was you. He's just too stubborn to see it. And you, you're just as stubborn. You think this ranch is it for you. You made a choice when you were injured. You married a man you loved, but you weren't in love with him. And then you lost him and you blamed yourself for that. You and Carson are doing a lot of the same things, but the difference is that you're a step ahead on the forgiving yourself part of the journey."

"Maybe so. And that's why I love you. You're always straight with me."

"I always will be. You're one of my kids."

"I'm going to go check on Eve. Do you need anything before I go?"

"I'm good. I have my pills, in case I have a spell. Isaac ran to the barn but he'll be back soon. Is Eve going to be okay?"

"Yes, she's just exhausted. We're trying some new exercises the physical therapist gave her, and they wear her out."

"Good deal. You let me know if she needs anything."

She got up, kissed the top of his head and left. As she walked across the lawn to her apartment she prayed for peace, she prayed for Carson and the children. She prayed she would know what God wanted from her, because she suddenly felt unsettled.

It was time to start a new chapter in her story. Over the years she'd become an expert at starting new chapters. This chapter would be about finding a way to get over missing Carson and his children.

She'd try her best to get over them. But she knew the truth.

This would be the most difficult chapter ever.

Chapter Seventeen

Carson opened the door to the hotel suite with a brilliant view of the Chicago skyline and led Andy and Maggie inside. It had been a long day. It had been a longer week. He'd applied for the job and had been turned down. A closed door. That's what Kylie would have told him. So if that door was closed, it meant God had opened another somewhere else. He'd sent out feelers at other hospitals and clinics. So far nothing.

They'd spent the day looking at homes. He'd made a spreadsheet of the best schools, the neighborhoods he was interested in and he'd searched houses closest to the schools. They'd also looked at a few apartments. Nothing they'd seen today looked like a place they could call home. But he wasn't giving up.

After house hunting, they'd gone by a few of the schools. Large, sterile places with locked doors and security. He understood; this was the city. In Dallas they'd lived in a suburb. Here, to be close to the special schools he wanted for Andy, they would have to be farther inside the city than they were used to.

Maggie had climbed up on the sofa with a book. He sat down next to her and stretched his legs out. His phone rang. He hoped it might be Kylie. He could tell her about the job search, the houses and all his doubts.

But it wasn't Kylie. He answered. "Hey, Colt, what are you up to?"

They hadn't talked in months. That was normal for them. Since Colt ran off at sixteen, they hadn't spent a lot of time talking. Colt had skipped college and opted for bullfighting school. He'd earned money in competitions and then he'd taken a job for the pro bull riding circuit. He told Carson not to worry about him.

"I'm standing in the lobby of this five-star hotel you're staying in, freezing my tail off and wondering if you'll give your brother a big old hug."

Carson laughed. "No hugs and the lobby has a rip-roaring fireplace."

"You wound me. And I just came in from outside where it's very cold."

"Come on up." He hung up and went to the door to wait.

"I miss my pony," Maggie randomly said as she looked through her book.

"You don't have a pony," Carson reminded her as he waited. "You have a dog named Rambo."

"I had a kitten. And Kylie. I like Eve, too."

"I know you do." Carson glanced at his watch. It was almost dinnertime. That meant another restaurant, another take-out meal or more room service. All of the options were starting to taste the same. They should have picked up bread and some bologna. Anything would be better than another meal prepared by a fancy chef.

Andy had settled on the floor with paper and crayons, Rambo stretched out next to him. "Andy, what do you want for dinner?"

"Eggs." He kept drawing. Carson grinned and it felt good, to find something amusing.

He could cook eggs. If he had eggs. The suite had a kitchen. He could get taco sauce. Andy liked taco sauce. He tried to remember what else Kylie had put in her eggs.

Kylie. She was on his mind a lot. Maybe because Andy and Maggie mentioned her daily, hourly, maybe more. It could be she was on his mind because he missed her.

A sharp knock on the door meant Colt had found them. He opened and motioned him inside. "Imagine seeing you in Chicago."

"Yeah, well, I thought I'd better take the opportunity while I can. You're hard to keep up with. Two weeks ago you were in Oklahoma."

Colt took off his hat and tossed it on a coffee table in the small living area. He sat on the sofa, close to Maggie. Rambo issue a low growl.

"Uncle Colt." Maggie wrapped her arms around his neck. "We got a dog. And almost a cat."

"How do you almost get a cat?"

"It's at Grandpa's with Kylie," Maggie whispered close to his ear. "It's gray."

"With Kylie, huh?"

"Stop," Carson warned.

Colt didn't even grin. "Anyway, I just thought I'd stop by and see how you all are doing. Daisy said you sounded sad to her. You don't look sad. You look like your normal serious self."

"Thanks." Carson sat down in a chair and studied his brother. "How do you know anything about Kylie?"

"I don't. I'm just guessing. You went to Hope. You saw Kylie at Jack's." Colt cleared his throat.

"You know Kylie lives at Mercy Ranch. Sounds like you've kept up with things a little better than I did."

"You had some kind of weird amnesia when we left. It was the trauma, I think. I'm not a therapist, but that would be my guess."

"Could be. So where are you off to next?"

"Jack's surgery is in two weeks," Colt said. "I guess I'll be there."

"That's good. He'd like that."

"It's more for me than him. I wouldn't be able to live with myself and all that nonsense."

"Right."

"Are you going?" Colt asked as he leaned to look at Andy's picture. "Hey, that's pretty good."

"Yes, I'm going."

"Good. I guess you don't want to work at Jack's clinic, then?"

"I guess you don't want to tell me how you know everything about everyone in Hope?"

Colt grinned and shook his head. His dark curly hair and dimples made him look more innocent than he'd ever been. "Not much to tell you. I've been to Hope. I have friends there."

"I didn't know that."

"No, you've kinda had other things on your mind the past few years. How are you?"

So they were going to be brotherly. It had been years since they'd had real conversation. Carson sat back, watching his children. Maggie with her book. Andy with his drawing.

"I'm good. I…" He stumbled over his words. But he pushed through. "I have days when I don't think of her. And I think of Kylie every single day."

"You've got to give yourself a break." Colt leaned back and chuckled. "Hey, Andy, what are you drawing there?"

Andy looked up, his expression serious. "Family."

"That's pretty awesome. Can you show your dad?"

Andy lifted the paper and showed it to Carson. Carson didn't know what to say. But Colt did. He laughed and slapped Carson on the back.

"Andy, that is just about the best drawing ever. See that, Carson? That's something you ought to frame."

"Yes, I probably should." Carson pulled out a dollar. "Can I have that picture when you get done? I'll trade you a dollar for it."

Andy nodded and went back to coloring. Carson watched as his son added a veil to the stick figure in the center of the picture and a cowboy hat to the figure standing next to her. Next he drew a stick figure boy and a smaller girl. A dog, it had to be a dog, sat next to the boy.

"What are you going to do, stick it on the fridge and tell yourself what a gutless wonder you are?" Colt asked as Carson watched his son finish the picture.

Carson had never hit a man before, but he considered hitting his younger brother. "I'm going to order pizza for dinner. Are you hungry?"

"Starving."

Carson took the picture to the kitchen and used a magnet to stick it on the refrigerator. He smiled at the image and wondered what Kylie would think.

Kylie caught Jack as he fell. She slid him to the floor of the stable office and yelled for help. He smiled up at her and whispered that she shouldn't worry.

"Be quiet, Jack. Don't tell me not to worry." She pulled the bottle of pills out of his pocket. "Jack, they're empty. Why are they empty?"

"Forgot."

"Call 911," she screamed. "Someone call an ambulance."

Isaac rushed through the door, followed by Matt. Jack had gone limp. "Help him," she whispered.

She ripped open his shirt and moved Isaac back. He was on the phone with the emergency dispatcher. She started chest compressions. When she got tired, Isaac took over. In the distance they could hear the ambulance. What was taking so long?

"Hurry, hurry, hurry," she prayed. "Come on, Jack."

The paramedics entered the room. Isaac pulled Kylie to her feet and held her as they worked. She watched as they used paddles to shock him.

"We have to call Carson," she whispered. She hadn't let herself think about him. But she knew that he'd want to know about Jack. She knew that she needed him here.

"I'll call," Isaac assured her. "I'm going to get the truck so we can follow the ambulance. I told them to take him to Grove but they're probably going to have to get him stable and send him to Tulsa."

She nodded, still numb. Still afraid they might lose Jack. She hated that he'd written up that stupid trust, as if he'd known this would happen. As if he feared he would leave loose ends.

Jack woke up briefly as they loaded him in the ambulance. He reached for Kylie and she took his hand. "We're calling Carson. We'll all be at the hospital."

He nodded. And she knew he mouthed that he loved her. "I love you, too. So get better."

Don't you dare die on me, she thought to herself.

Isaac pulled up with the truck. "Get in. I called Carson. He said Colt is staying with him for a few days. They'll head this way together. Daisy is living in Tulsa."

Kylie got in the truck and closed her eyes.

"Pray out loud," Isaac said. "I need to hear some prayers."

She prayed and prayed. And then she cried.

"I know he's your father, but he's the closest I have to one." She wiped at her eyes. "And that's really selfish of me. I'm so sorry, Isaac."

"It's okay. Hang in there, Kylie. He's too tough to die on us."

It took thirty minutes to get to Grove, and that meant going over the speed limit at times. Kylie kept her mouth shut. She wanted to get there as badly as Isaac did.

When they pulled in to the hospital, a nurse met them. Kylie began to shake.

"He has to be okay," she whispered.

"We have doctors with him right now," the nurse assured her as she led them to a small consultation room. "He's conscious. We're going to stabilize him and send him to Tulsa. That's where you want him, right?"

Isaac nodded. The nurse focused on him. "Are you next of kin?"

"Yes. I'm his son."

"Does he have a DNR?" she asked.

Isaac looked lost. "I have no idea." He looked at Kylie.

She shook her head. "He doesn't."

Isaac's hand went to his face, covering his eyes. Kylie put an arm around him and tried to be the person he could rely on. Falling apart wouldn't do them or Jack any good.

"Would you like to see him?" the nurse offered.

"Yes, please." Isaac stood and followed her to the door. He turned to wait for Kylie.

"I think you should go." She joined him at the door. "Isaac, I'll see him before he leaves. You should go to him now."

"Okay. When I'm done, you're going in."

She was in the waiting room when he returned. He sat down next to her and buried his face in his hands. "I've never seen him like this before."

Kylie put a hand on his back. "Were you able to talk to him?"

"Yes. He's awake. You should go in."

She got up and slowly made her way through the doors of the emergency room. A nurse pointed her in the right direction. Jack's eyes caught hers as she entered the room.

"You gave me a scare."

"Sorry." His voice shook and she had a difficult time hearing him. "I'm good. Carson?"

"We called them."

"Good. You two."

"Nope. Not right now." She squeezed his hand and he squeezed back, but weaker than he'd ever been before. She was so used to him being strong.

"Yes," he said. Stubborn man.

"Jack, everything will be fine. I know it. In my heart I know you're going to be fine."

"Me, too."

And then they arrived to start the transport and she was asked to leave. She told Jack she'd see him in Tulsa. As she walked through the hospital, she realized she needed coffee. Isaac would probably like a cup, too. There had to be a vending machine nearby. She just needed a few minutes to compose herself.

She saw Donnie standing at the end of a hall; a sign midway down pointed to the cafeteria. "Donnie. What are you doing here? Is everything okay?"

And then she saw the police officer on the floor, a dark bruise on his forehead. "Donnie, we have to get him help."

"Not on your life." Donnie grabbed her as she turned to run.

Chapter Eighteen

Carson and Colt headed down the hall to the room number they'd been given. Daisy had remained in the waiting room with Maggie and Andy. She wasn't quite ready to see their father. Carson entered the room first; Colt came in behind him. Isaac stood to greet them, shaking Carson's hand first and then Colt's.

Carson guessed he should make the introductions. "Colt, this is our brother Isaac."

"Guess I should say its good to meet you. Not exactly how I would normally greet a sibling." Colt moved to the bed and looked down at the pale, sleeping form of their father. "How is he?"

"Better. Stable and they're talking about doing the open heart surgery next week. They want him a little stronger before they open him up."

"Has the doctor been in today?" Carson asked.

"Yeah, he was here." Isaac pointed to a chair. "One of you can sit. I need to stand for a while."

"I'll sit." Colt didn't mind taking the only chair in the room. Carson had to give his brother credit. Very little bothered Colt.

Jack's eyes opened. "Carson. Isaac, does he know?"

Isaac shook his head. "No, I'll tell him."

"Know what?" Carson stepped closer to the bed. "That you're stubborn and having your surgery a little sooner than you would have liked? Colt's here."

Jack turned his head to face Colt. "Hello, stranger."

Colt came to his feet and moved to the side of the bed. "You gave us a scare but I'm glad you decided to hang around."

"Me, too." Again Jack turned to Isaac. "Tell him."

Isaac motioned to the door and Carson followed. "What's going on?"

"It's Kylie." Isaac blew out a breath in obvious frustration. "Man, Carson, I just… He was there and we didn't know."

"What are you talking about?"

"Donnie was at the hospital yesterday. Kylie left Jack and went looking for coffee but she met up with Donnie. He'd knocked out the cop who had him in custody. She tried to run but

Donnie grabbed her. Fortunately the cop came to and used a stun gun on him. It could have been worse. He planned on taking her hostage."

"Where is she?" Carson knocked Isaac's hands off him. "Is she here?"

"No." Isaac pushed him up against the wall and held him there. "She's in Grove at the hospital there. She has a broken arm and she had a pretty good concussion. They're keeping her for a couple of days."

"I have to go." Carson walked back to his father's room. "Jack, I have to go."

"I know you do." Jack reached for his hand. "Take care of her."

"I will." He should have been there. He never should have left.

Colt followed him from the room and stopped him in the hall. "You didn't do this."

"What?"

"That look on your face. Put away the guilt and go take care of Kylie. You ought to pull that picture out of your wallet and show it to her."

The picture. He'd forgotten. "I'll take the rental car. You all can ride with Isaac."

"Sure thing, bro. When you get there, let me know how things go. You know, I'm in that picture, too, and I think I'm the guy in the suit next to you."

"Yeah, I doubt it." It had felt good to joke but

as he loaded the kids in the rental car, the fear washed over him again.

For the last few years he hadn't prayed much. But then he'd gone back to Hope, and prayer seemed like the right thing to do. Not only did he pray for Kylie's healing, he prayed that she would see a way to forgive a man whose heart had a few scars but was healing nicely.

When he walked into her room, she was sleeping. He sat down on the chair next to her bed and pulled Maggie and Andy onto his lap. Rambo stood on his hind legs and put his paws on the bed, whining as he looked at her lying there. Silent. Still. Carson didn't blame the dog. He felt a lot like whining, too. Her face was bruised. Her arm was in a cast. She moaned quietly in her sleep.

Carson waited until her eyes flickered open and she saw him. A pained smile shifted her mouth and then she grimaced. "What are you doing here? You should be in Tulsa."

"Jack disagreed. He said I needed to be here. And Rambo missed you. He asked if he could come home."

"He can't come home. He's Andy's dog now."

"I see." Carson sat there a moment, studying her face. "I guess you don't get a say in the matter. You obviously need a service dog. It would do you a lot of good."

"I have Skip," she whispered. "I need water."

He got up and set the kids down in the chair. He raised her slightly and lifted the mug of water to her lips. She drank and then smiled up at him. "I missed you."

"We missed you, too."

He pulled his wallet out of his pocket. "I meant to get this framed but for some reason I stuck it in my pocket."

He unfolded the picture that Andy had drawn the first night of Colt's visit.

"What is it?"

He looked at it and grinned. "I think it might be our invitation."

"Invitation?" she asked as she reached for the paper that he kept just out of reach.

He turned the picture sideways and then long ways again. He smiled at her over the top of the sheet of paper.

"Carson?" She giggled a little. "What are you doing?"

"I'm trying to do this, but Rambo is in my way. He kind of assumed the position I had hoped for."

"Whining at the side of my bed?"

"No, not really."

Maggie began to laugh. "It's Andy's picture of Kylie."

"A picture of me?"

"No." Carson looked at it.

"Show me?" she pleaded.

"I think it's the story of us." He placed the picture in her hands and then he moved Rambo over and took his place, kneeling at the side of the bed. "I believe in puppy love, but that dog has to find his own girlfriend."

Kylie laughed and cried as she looked at the picture and the man at the side of her bed, down on one knee. Tears streamed down her cheeks as she realized this was their story. She lifted the picture and smiled at the version of their lives that had been drawn by a little boy not quite five who obviously wanted his own family.

The stick figures in the drawing done in brown and green crayon were obviously their family. A dog, a boy and girl, a few cowboys in very large hats and a grandpa with gray hair. But in the center of all of those people was a couple and she wore a dress, he wore a tie. It looked like a picture of a very happy ending.

"Get up off the floor," she told Carson as she held the picture to her cheek. "This is all I need."

"No, you need more." Carson touched the

fingers that stuck out of the cast. She had just painted her nails. That stupid Donnie had messed up her manicure. He'd bruised her hip. He had really ruined her day.

"What more do I need?" she asked.

"A proposal. Once, a long time ago, a thirteen-year-old boy loved the prettiest girl in Oklahoma. And then he left and life took them both down different paths."

"Until they met again years later only to find she'd been sleeping for twenty years, waiting for him."

"But he kissed her." Carson stood up, and she couldn't help but hold her breath as their gazes clashed and he leaned in. "Is this appropriate?"

She nodded. "I think so. We have chaperones."

He captured her lips for a quick but sweet kiss. "He kissed her, and promised to kiss her more. Every day if she would like. For the rest of their lives."

"Daddy," Maggie giggled. "Don't do that."

"Marry me," he said. "Let's make this story complete. Marry me and raise my children with me. I love you, Kylie. We know each other's secrets, faults, heartaches. But we can surely find other things to discover."

"I don't want to live in Chicago." She shrugged

as she felt tears burn behind her eyes, hoping he would understand.

"That's good because we don't want to live in Chicago either."

Maggie clapped her hands. "We want ponies and kittens."

Andy slid out of the chair and moved to the bed. "I miss you."

That did it. Tears streamed down her face. "Carson, hold that child up here so I can kiss his cheeks."

Carson lifted first Andy for a hug and kiss and then he lifted Maggie. But Maggie had other plans. She slid from his hands and cuddled against Kylie's good side. And it felt so good to have her there.

"I hope that clinic is still empty. I'm going to need a job."

"I think your dad has been saving it for you, hoping you would come to your senses."

"It took a while but I got here. Finally."

"I love you, Carson. And I love our family."

Epilogue

They had the picture Andy had drawn framed, but first they had copied it and created their wedding invitation:

> Jack West would like to invite you to the wedding of his son Carson West to his soon-to-be daughter, Kylie Adams. The ceremony will take place on the Fifth day of May at First Church of Hope. No gifts please. Donations can be made to the Wounded Warrior fund or your local VA.

Kylie stood in the church vestibule with Jack, because he insisted on being the man who gave her away. She smiled at the procession going before her. Daisy and Isaac, Eve and Colt, although Colt seemed to be looking for someone in the pews and Eve was avoiding looking at Jaxon.

Andy and Rambo were the ring bearers; the ring was attached to a pillow on Rambo's collar. Maggie was the prettiest flower girl ever with her blond curly hair and big brown eyes. She tossed the pink rose petals as she sang to herself.

It was perfect. It was the wedding she'd once dreamed of, more than twenty years ago when two thirteen-year-old kids thought they were in love.

Now they knew the truth. It was definitely love.

Jack squeezed her arm. "You ready to make this journey?"

"I'm more than ready," she said, leaning briefly against his shoulder.

The wedding march began to play and Jack walked her down the aisle to her groom. Carson took a deep breath as she came to stand beside him.

"You know I love you," he whispered in her ear.

"I love you more and more every day," she replied.

"Could we start the ceremony?" The pastor smiled as he asked. "Because we can wait if you all have something you want to share with everyone."

"No, I think they all know what we want to say." Carson took her hand in his.

"You don't hold hands until I tell you," the pastor reminded. "It's part of the ceremony."

"The ceremony is taking a long time." Maggie yawned and then tossed more flowers.

Everyone laughed.

The pastor began. "This is the story of a couple who found each other, lost each other and found each other again. It's a story of a couple that found faith, went through the fire and came out on the other side refined as gold.

"They will go through amazing times, loss, heartache, joy and tribulation, only to go through it all again. Because this is life. It isn't perfect. It's guaranteed to be messy. But somehow this couple will survive."

Carson and Kylie beamed at each other, but truthfully she just wanted him to kiss her. She wanted to walk out of this church, her hand in his, knowing that their story didn't end here. It was a whole new beginning for them all.

They would be one family. Forever.

* * * * *

If you loved this story,
be sure to check out the miniseries
Bluebonnet Springs

Second Chance Rancher
The Rancher's Christmas Bride
The Rancher's Secret Child

from bestselling author Brenda Minton

Available now from Love Inspired!

Find more great reads at
www.LoveInspired.com

Dear Reader,

I hope you enjoy the first book in the Mercy Ranch series. Mercy Ranch and the characters who live there are already favorites of mine, and I hope they'll quickly become your favorites, too.

Carson and Kylie share a very broken past and they come together still searching for a way to put their lives back together. What they find as they try to maintain their separate lives is that God has always had a plan for the two of them. And that plan has brought them both to Mercy Ranch!

Thank you for taking this journey with me to Oklahoma. I continue to be uplifted by your many emails, messages and kind words.

Blessings,
Brenda